Those
Snake Island Kids

Jon Tucker

Illustrated by the author
(with help from some of those kids)

Also by Jon Tucker

Snow Petrel
Those Eco-Pirate Kids
Those Shipwreck Kids

 For more information,
visit www.nzmaid.com

First published in 2012 by Forty Degrees South
This edition 2017 by Storm Bay Books
© Jon Tucker 2012

ISBN 978-0-9808353-4-2

Also available as an ebook
ISBN 978-0-9808353-1-1

Proudly produced by APM Publishing Services: 0428 232 717

When Jake persuades his family to embark on a sailing-camping holiday on an island in Tasmania, he is mostly interested in pirate fantasies and his home-built sailing dinghy.

But he does not plan on events which are to leave him isolated with his brother and sister, and a couple of Kiwi kids. Ultimately, after being forced to dig deep into their personal reserves, the treasures they all gain from their experiences are very different from the ones Jake has set out to find.

This uplifting tale of youthful naivety, camaraderie, calamity and triumph will appeal to any free-spirited reader in the nine to ninety-nine age bracket.

About the Author

Jon Tucker is a Kiwi ex-teacher turned adventurer whose piratical black ketch is the only home he and his wife Barbara owned for most of their lives. They and their five sons extensively sailed the waters of New Zealand, Australia and the Pacific. Their accumulated experiences have provided Jon with sufficient material, both true and imaginative, to begin a linked series of children's books.

Author's Note

Although this is essentially a work of fiction, it is based on true events and real places. Snake Island exists, uninhabited, exactly as on Jess's maps. The historical details are accurate, treasure hunters are still looking for the missing gold, and even the story of a group of teenage campers being marooned during a storm is real.

As for the lifestyle of the Kiwi twins – my own Kiwi children have lived exactly this way, sailing off for a year or longer with all their schoolwork in boxes, plotting expeditions, camping on deserted islands and living a lifestyle inspired by Arthur Ransome's 'Swallows and Amazon' kids.

And although the forty-spots' existence still hangs in the balance, thanks to the work of so many concerned bird-lovers, there remains hope for their future.

Contents

List of Illustrations

Maps:

Illustrations:

To Ron, Pat, Fred and Joc for beginning the adventure
A.R. for inspiring it
Ben, Dan, Josh, Sam and Matt for living it
And most of all to Babs for making it happen

The Channel

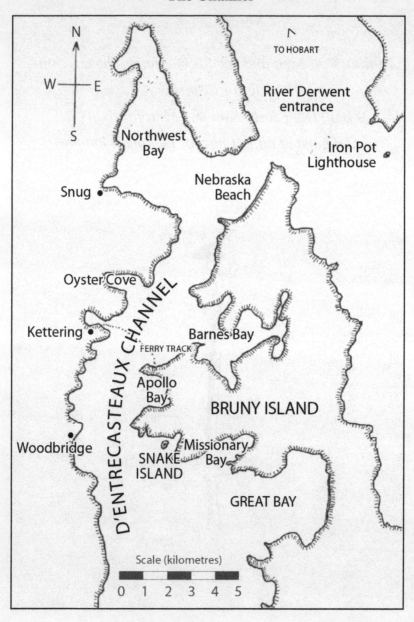

Chapter 1

Privateer

JAKE HAD BUILT HIS OWN pirate ship and tomorrow would be sailing it to a deserted island. At least he hoped it would be deserted. Not like last time, when there were a mob of kayakers having a picnic.

It was only a little ship, but when you are Jake's age you don't need a particularly big boat. Grandma had told him that any sailing boat deserved to be called a ship, even a small Optimist sailing dinghy like his.

It was only a small island too. But Jake had his own secret theory about Snake Island. Ever since he'd seen that red-bearded kayaker with his map covered in crosses, Jake had been searching the internet for shipwreck stories. Now he had his answer, but had told nobody yet about his plans to do a little digging ...

If only he could get to sleep. The house was quiet after all the noisy packing. Even Mum and Dad were asleep. For months he had been planning this holiday, and at last it was nearly happening. Jake pictured himself pushing off from the dock with his cargo of camping gear. Jess would probably make some comment about his sails not setting properly, and Fin might be pestering him to come too with a fishing lure. But no, on this first

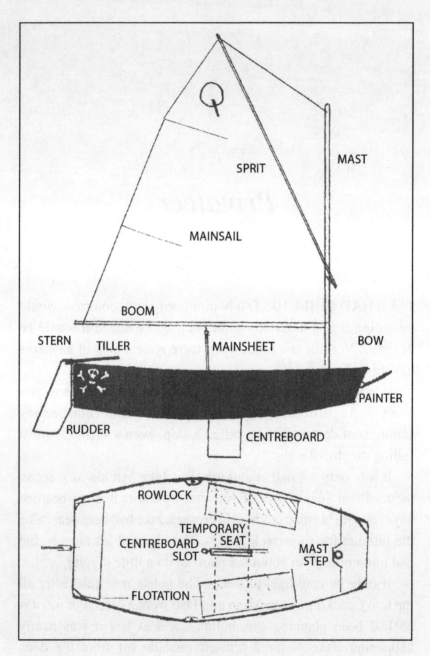

Privateer

voyage he would be a solo skipper.

Thinking back, Jake recalled finding the Optimist plans on the web. He remembered the long hours spent boatbuilding in the garage and those afternoons rushing home from school to see if the glue had dried. And then the weekends of sanding and painting.

"But it was all my own work", he thought proudly. "Okay, Dad did help quite a lot and lent me his tools, but no-one can say it's not totally mine. There's probably no other boat in the world quite the same."

It looked so awesome painted black, with its gold skull and crossbones on each side. And the pirate name too. He had originally wanted a black sail, but that wasn't so easy. Grandma had paid for the sail as a birthday present, but black sail-cloth is hard to get so in the end it had to be red. He would still look right with a blood red sail and a black dinghy. 'Black Jake' he would call himself, the 'Terror of the Channel'.

Grandma had been a great support. It was probably the stories she told about her childhood adventures, camping and sailing in England, that had first given him the idea of building his own boat. She knew how hard he had saved to buy plywood, and how he had earned extra money mowing neighbours' lawns. Sometimes it seemed that she was as excited as him about the boat, so he had promised to take her for a sail aboard *Privateer* as soon as he was confident.

Jake knew the bays and islands of this part of Tasmania reasonably well already. During the past three years the family had sailed their nine metre H28 sloop all through the D'Entrecasteaux Channel and as far north as Wineglass Bay. Jake's favourite part was the swing-bridge and canal at Dunalley. Jess loved the passage near the Iron Pot lighthouse where she could take compass bearings and cover the chart with pencil lines. Fin's favourite area was south of Maria Island where the fishing was best. He had caught a big albacore tuna there last summer and had pestered Mum and Dad hard this year to go back. But no, Jake eventually persuaded everyone that a sailing-camping week at Snake Island would be the most fun.

"Aw come on", he had argued, "if us kids can camp ashore it'll be heaps more comfortable for Mum and Dad."

Everyone knew that his main reason was more about pirates and deserted islands, but Mum and Dad had privately agreed about the chance for more peaceful mornings. Jess had quickly realised that it would be fun to practise navigation by mapping the island, and Fin had seen the opportunity to catch a king flathead at the Snake Island reef from the dinghy.

As he lay, still awake, Jake thought back over the evening's noisy preparations. Mum was the most organised of course. She had bought all the boat food and supplies several days earlier and had done most of the camp food shopping for the three kids that afternoon. Fin was mostly focussed on his precious fishing gear. Jess had carefully packed her technical drawing equipment into a big plastic bag along with her orienteering compass and several large sheets of paper. Jake had been more secretive about his private hoard which included a large pirate flag, various pieces of rope and string, a cheap blue tarpaulin, an old machete (next best thing to a cutlass) and a folding shovel.

It was the thought of wandering through the undergrowth of a deserted island that finally helped Jake relax, and his next conscious moment was the sound of his younger brother calling him for breakfast.

THE VILLAGE OF Kettering, forty minutes' drive south of Hobart, is crowded with boats – mostly older yachts and launches.

Jim and Rose Brownrig had chosen to keep their slightly scruffy blue H28 yacht here so that they could sail *Sea Fever* with their children easily into any number of safe anchorages in the channel without having to spend three hours sailing down the Derwent River from Hobart.

Jim was particularly fond of Bruny Island which sprawled its way southwards towards the bottom corner of Tasmania. It created a sheltered waterway, perfect for weekend cruising. His wife Rose had grown up sailing small boats in England, and it had been her idea originally to buy *Sea Fever* and get the children away from the virtual worlds of computers.

As he drove down the channel highway towards Kettering that morning, Jim was on top of the world. Rose was busy talking with the older two children about camp cooking, and Fin was counting hooks and sinkers, humming to himself. As he thought back over the past year, Jim felt proud of his children. Jess was growing up to be such a confident girl, and Jake had done a great job of building his sailing dinghy. Jim glanced in the rear view mirror to confirm that the little black Optimist was still tied safely in the trailer, loaded up with enough camping gear to nearly sink poor *Sea Fever*.

LOOKING DOWN FROM the balcony of the Kettering café which serves tourists and locals as they wait for the car ferry to Bruny Island, it is easy to see the activities at the small marina below. On this particular summer morning the most entertaining sight for one group of tourists was a blue yacht being loaded for what was obviously a family holiday. How all that gear could possibly fit into such a smallish yacht was anyone's guess. The father with his scruffy mop of springy hair seemed to be

Before the launching

uncertain where to stow the growing mountain of bags and had started fiddling with ropes beside the mast. Meanwhile the mother was organising the children to pass certain things here and fit others there.

A moment later and the two bigger children could be seen carrying a small black sailing dinghy along the walkway and preparing to put it into the water. A smaller boy was following with a red sail wrapped neatly in three poles, one of which was probably a mast. The whole family was soon involved, lowering the dinghy into the water as the bigger boy poured what looked like cola soft drink over the front and the others clapped. The watching tourists expected to see the red sail rigged, but instead the boy produced what looked like a seat and fitted it over the centreboard slot. His sister handed him two oars and he rowed uncertainly away, looking slightly uncomfortable but making good progress. He called something back to the father about his knees being too high, before rowing back alongside the blue sloop.

A noisy flurry of propeller wash from the returning ferry distracted the tourists. There was coffee to finish, and they soon hurried away to the car queue, leaving the blue boat family to the privacy they preferred.

FOR THE FAMILY aboard *Sea Fever*, the big decision was whether to tow some of the camping gear behind them, particularly the three heavy water containers which were too difficult to stow on the floor of the already overloaded cabin. They could be put easily enough in the yacht's big dinghy, a three metre fibreglass rowing boat.

"I'm taking a tent and bedroll in *Privateer*," stated Jake.

"No way!" Jess reacted immediately. "It's impossible to dry things if they get salty. Remember our clothes when we capsized the dinghy at Wineglass Bay?"

"You're right Jess," agreed her mother. "It's going to be bad enough getting used to your new boat today Jake, without having cargo to trim."

It was after midday by the time the last of the stores was aboard. Jake was anxious to set sail, as the first breath of an easterly sea-breeze was stirring the water and he was keen to tack his way nearer to the shelter of Bruny Island before it kicked up too much of a choppy sea.

"Don't be too proud to stop and let us tow *Privateer*, Jake," said his father as Jake hastily munched a tomato and cheese sandwich. "And remember that you can reduce sail to half its area by letting go the sprit. It's not very good for the sail but it's better than being over-canvassed."

"I know," replied Jake, thinking back to the Optimist sailing course he had done last summer, learning tricks like sailing backwards and swimming inside an upturned dinghy to breathe the air in the spooky green light inside.

"Signal us if you want a tow. And keep the painter in reach so you can tie a longer rope to it. We can pull you alongside and get the mast out."

Jake fumbled a little as he rigged the tiller and set up the sprit until the sail set without a wrinkle. *Privateer* had been alongside *Sea Fever* since the morning's rowing trial. Now, as he pushed off and drifted back into the clear water between the marina piles, he waved and concentrated, forgetting completely that he was Black Jake, Terror of the Channel. Behind him he heard the familiar chug-chug of *Sea Fever*'s diesel engine increase in pitch as her lines were cast off, and she transformed into a mother ship accompanying a solo sailor to a deserted island.

Chapter 2

Maiden Solo Voyage

JESS'S FAVOURITE TV PROGRAMME WAS 'Sea Patrol'. She imagined herself as the navigator aboard a navy ship's bridge, her ponytail poking out from under her cap, peering intently at the radar and plotter, and poring over charts of coral-studded waters. Today, as she cast off the mooring lines while *Sea Fever* reversed out of the marina berth, she couldn't help herself calling the correct response to her father at the stern.

"Lines away, Sir," she shouted in best naval fashion. "Standing by for further orders!"

"Maintain lookout ahead," responded her father good-naturedly. He didn't look much like a captain with his shorts and tee-shirt and scruffy hair, she thought privately, smiling to herself as she scanned the waters around her. Just ahead to starboard was Jake in his smart black dinghy, slipping along nicely with his red sail pulled in tight as he tacked out of the bay. Jess had to admit that he deserved a successful first voyage after all the effort he had put into building the Optimist last year. Away to their port side was a white two masted yacht, bigger than *Sea Fever*. A large flag flew off a flagstaff at the stern.

"Permission to come aft, Sir?" she called to her father,

anxious to get the binoculars for a better look. But Fin had beaten her to it, and by the time she had sidled down the side-deck, he was examining the white yacht intently.

"There are two kids aboard," he said. "And it's got a foreign flag."

"I can't see it properly," complained Jess. "Let me have a look."

"It's quite like the Australian flag but it doesn't have the big white star and its stars are red. They look like the Southern Cross," continued Fin, determinedly clutching the binoculars.

"It'll be a New Zealand yacht then," said his father. "If you look hard you might see a small courtesy flag flying at the spreaders."

Australia   *New Zealand*

By now Jess had wrestled the binoculars from her younger brother and, feeling very much the navigator again, focused on the white yacht. True to her father's word, she could see a tiny Australian flag fluttering from the rigging halfway up the mainmast. She switched her gaze to two children sitting reading in the cockpit.

"Tradition says that the flag of the country you are visiting should be higher than your own flag," her father continued, "even if it's smaller."

But Jess wasn't listening. She was examining the two overseas kids, choking back a feeling of envy as she wondered what it would be like to cross the Tasman Sea on a yacht. Fin meanwhile was more interested in the small grey inflatable dinghy tied to its stern.

"Lucky pigs! Wish we had an inflatable like that. It'd be so much quicker getting to fishing spots."

"Yes but think of how much petrol you'd burn," retorted his mother as she gathered up the cups from the cockpit. "Watch out for the ferry Jim," she added as she disappeared down the hatch. The Bruny Island car ferry was entering the bay ahead, and her husband altered course to steer away from its path. "How's Jake doing – is he keeping out of the ferry's way?" At that very moment Jess saw the little red sail swing across as her brother tacked to keep clear of the big blue ferry and the rough wake behind it.

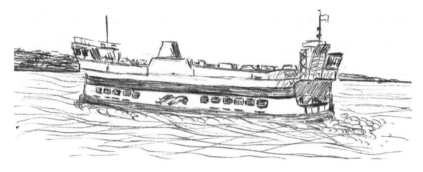

"Yep, he's okay." And remembering to be the navigator again, she dived below into the chaos of stores to fetch her compass. As soon as she was back on deck she began taking a series of compass bearings to check angles between *Sea Fever* and the ferry.

"What are you doing now Jess?" asked Fin. He knew she enjoyed explaining her superior skills, and it sometimes helped to get on her good side.

"Checking our relative bearing," she explained, pleased to be asked. "If the angle between two boats stays the same then they are probably going to collide."

"So what's the verdict Jess?" asked her father, already knowing the answer.

"Zero collision risk, sir. Maintain present course."

"That's a relief!" he replied. "Okay Fin, take the helm and we'll get some sail up."

"Aye aye, Dad." Grasping the tiller as he often had before, Fin looked for a distant headland of Bruny Island to steer towards while his father and sister let go the sail ties on the mainsail.

SITTING MUCH CLOSER to the water and waves than his younger brother, Jake was also grasping a tiller. The sea-breeze was steadily increasing, and he had tacked twice already. There was less time to look about, and though he had noticed the overseas yacht anchored on the north side of the bay, he was more intent on the approaching ferry. He hoped this would be the last starboard tack, as he should soon be able to point *Privateer* directly for Apollo Bay on Bruny Island where there would be better shelter.

A splash of spray slopped over the bow, and he glanced at the varnished plywood floor. A small puddle of brown liquid had already collected there, a reminder of his little launching ceremony only two hours earlier. He had wanted to christen the boat with rum, the pirate way, but Dad wouldn't let any of his precious rum go to waste. "Why not use coke," he had suggested. "After all, it's what we mix with rum!" So coke it had been. Pity Grandma hadn't come down for the launching. She had said she would, but she hadn't been very well lately and now he would have to wait until they got back to show her the new red sail.

As the ferry passed, he tacked over again, and soon hit its wake, a series of steep little waves. For a few seconds *Privateer* became a bucking bronco, with quite a lot more spray splashing over the bows.

Sea Fever was gaining on him now. He could see the mainsail

Maiden solo voyage

being pulled up, and wondered how far ahead they would get before they slowed down for him. The sea-breeze was already blowing quite hard and Jake wondered if it would get much stronger today. He tried to remember what his father had told him about this type of breeze. Something about the difference between land and sea temperatures. It's a bit cloudy today, he reasoned, so the land shouldn't get too hot and maybe it won't get much stronger.

Jake didn't want it any stronger either. By the time he was halfway across the channel with his sail sheeted hard in, regular splashes of water were slopping over the port side near the bow. His shorts were quite wet already, and he felt a little uncertain of himself. *Privateer* seemed very small now, and it was a long way from land here, maybe even a kilometre, he judged. He'd never been this far from land in the club Optimists when he was learning to sail. And there had always been an instructor in a fast inflatable nearby, yelling encouragement.

Ahead he suddenly noticed a large fin waving in the air. It was only about ten boat-lengths away and Jake felt a brief rush of terror, instinctively pulling the tiller to steer away. But looking closer he could see it was no giant shark fin, only a flipper waving in the air as a fat seal rolled lazily in the water. They often saw seals around here, attracted by the salmon farms, but it took a while before Jake's nerves had steadied.

Feeling small and quite exposed, Jake was no longer the pirate he had intended to be. The spray had washed some sunscreen into his eyes and they were stinging even worse as he rubbed them. His lifejacket was scratching the back of his neck, and his right hand was becoming cramped from gripping the tiller so tightly. He baled out a dozen scoops of water and fought back the urge to wave to *Sea Fever* for a tow. Gritting his teeth, he concentrated even harder on reaching the more sheltered waters near Bruny Island.

A HUNDRED METRES ahead, aboard *Sea Fever*, his mother was steering now. Rose was pleased to be finally on the helm after the stresses of holiday preparations, and Fin had wanted a chance to get a fishing lure over the stern in case there were any Australian salmon or barracouta around. Her husband was hovering, keeping a regular eye behind them on Jake through the binoculars. Jess had her nose in her Small Boat Skipper manual, trying to memorise the shape and colour of navigation marker buoys.

"He seems to be coping okay so far," Jim stated. "It's the roughest he's ever sailed in a dinghy, so we still might have to go back for him. And Fin, if we do turn around, I want you to pull that fishing line in straight away. We don't want the propeller getting a line tangled in it."

Jess looked up from her manual, thinking of the time at Maria Island when Dad had to dive to cut a fishing line away from the propeller. The nylon had melted into a solid ring of plastic around the stainless steel shaft, and there had been a terrible grinding noise when Dad had put the engine into gear.

Thirty more minutes passed, comfortably enough for the Brownrig crew aboard their sloop, but considerably worse for the 'Terror of the Channel' a few hundred metres astern. Much to Jake's relief the choppy water began at last to flatten out as he approached the land ahead. Close to the headland near Apollo Bay the wind almost died away, and Rose eased out the mainsail so that Jake could catch up.

"Well done," called his father, "but it'll be three o'clock soon and the worst bit's still ahead."

Jake could see what his father meant. The sea-breeze had not really died, but was simply blowing harder ahead, across the open waters of Great Bay, where the land was acting like a giant wind funnel. He could see white-capped waves racing past the headland only two hundred metres away.

"Okay Dad," he called back. "We might as well tow her the rest of the way." He knew that Jess and Fin would be getting impatient to set up camp, and secretly he didn't know if he had the nerve for an even harder bash into the wind and waves between here and Snake Island.

Using his best seamanship skills, Jake manoevred alongside the familiar blue topsides where eager hands clutched his mast and took his painter. It was easy enough in these calm waters for him to pull out the mast, rudder and centreboard and climb aboard, tying *Privateer* a long way astern clear of the bigger white dinghy.

The rest of the trip was a familiar routine. The Brownrig kids knew the drill well enough. Their father decided to motor with the mainsail sheeted tight to save having to tack around the salmon farm that took up a large area of water to the south of Snake Island.

As they drew near to the deserted island their mood grew more excited. Despite catching no fish, Fin was happy to pull in his lure again while Jake scanned the island with the binoculars. Jess was taking a compass bearing on the marker pole at the end of the long reef to the south of the island.

Jess the navigator takes a compass sight

"It's a south cardinal mark," she was trying to explain, although nobody seemed to be taking much notice. "See how the triangles both point down. It's safe to go around its south side."

"I don't reckon there's anyone on the island," said Jake with satisfaction.

"Let me have them now. You've had them long enough!" Fin was having his usual struggle to get a chance to use the binoculars.

"Time all you crew got the mainsail down and stowed," interrupted their mother. "You can't abandon us until we're fully shipshape!"

As *Sea Fever* motored the last few hundred metres into the anchorage to the east of the island, the choppy seas calmed down again while all hands worked eagerly to stow sails and help with anchoring. And now that the galley had stopped bouncing and rolling, the offer of a snack before going ashore was welcomed by all three of the eager young shore party.

Snake Island

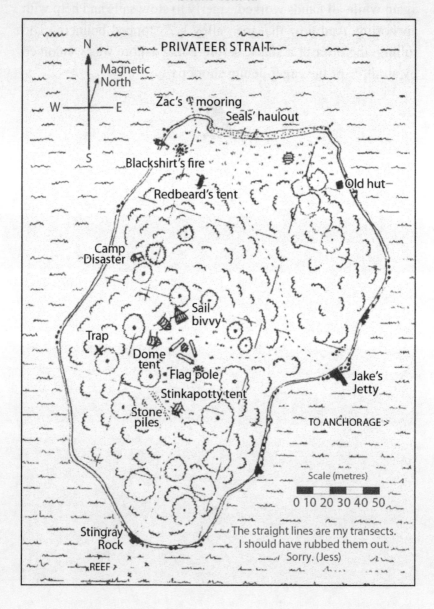

PRIVATEER STRAIT

N

Magnetic North

W   E

S

Zac's mooring

Seals' haulout

Blackshirt's fire

Redbeard's tent

Old hut

Camp Disaster

Sail bivvy

Trap

Dome tent

Flag pole

Jake's Jetty

Stinkapotty tent

TO ANCHORAGE >

Stone piles

Scale (metres)

0 10 20 30 40 50

Stingray Rock

The straight lines are my transects.
I should have rubbed them out.
Sorry. (Jess)

REEF >

Chapter 3

Marooned at Last

IT TOOK A LOT OF talking to convince their parents not to come ashore and help. Jake and Jess were both determined that the shore party should be left to itself without any interference.

"I've done this before on Duke of Ed trips," argued Jess, referring to her school-based bushwalking camps.

"I've done heaps of camping too," added Jake. "You'll spoil it if you come and interfere."

Their parents knew better than to argue. Deep down it was mostly the enjoyment of being involved themselves in a camping holiday that made them want to help.

"Okay, do it your way then," grumbled their mother good-naturedly. "But take your mobile phone, Jess, and remember that you can call us for help any time. Is it in range here? And is it charged up?"

Jess pulled it from her pocket and studied it briefly. "It's got one bar up so I should get out okay. Otherwise I could still text. I charged it last night so it'll be good for a couple of days."

"Can I take the hand-held?" asked Jake, referring to the portable VHF marine radio they sometimes used between ship and shore. He wished he had a mobile of his own, but his parents had insisted last year that he couldn't afford the cost of calls while he was pouring all his spare money into boatbuilding expenses.

"I don't think you'll need it tonight really," said his father. "If you leave it switched on all night the batteries will go flat and anyway you can probably yell from the shore to here."

"I'm taking a flag for a signal," added Fin. "Just in case we need help and the mobile doesn't work. I'll get the red protest flag from the locker."

"You can come and see our camp after tea," added Jake, not wanting his parents to feel left out.

It was low tide when they rowed ashore for the first time. Jake insisted on putting all his personal gear into *Privateer*, while Jess and Fin loaded up the bigger fibreglass dinghy. They had to bale and sponge out the bottom of both boats before loading, and even then they were careful to keep important things like sleeping bags and Jess's map-making folder off the damp areas. Fin wanted to sit at the bow to be ready to jump ashore with the painter, but Jess found it impossible to row with the stern so high, so they had to go back and rearrange the heavy items to help the dinghy balance.

Meanwhile Jake had already set up *Privateer* with its rowing seat slotted into the centreboard case (his father's invention) and was rowing awkwardly ashore to find a good landing place.

"It's harder to row than a normal dinghy," he called to his parents. "The seat's so high and it feels like I'm rowing a big saucer. But it's better than trying to paddle it like a canoe." As he neared the shore he began to regret his haste. The whole eastern shore was very rocky, with some big slabs angling down into the water, some crusted with nasty looking sharp oyster shells. Jake realised very quickly that *Privateer*'s beautiful new paint would be badly scraped if he tried to row alongside one of these rocks without someone to help hold him off and unload.

One rock outcrop extended further out than the others and had good deep water next to it. Looking back he saw the bigger dinghy approaching, so taking on the role of pirate captain in the advance party's jollyboat, he called instructions to the approaching longboat. "Over here. It's like a stone jetty. Probably not so good at high tide but it's perfect now for unloading. Keep a lookout for any hostile savages Fin."

Fin ignored the pirate command and scrambled ashore to tie the painter around a rock. With some difficulty Jess gripped the rock as the heavy dinghy moved with the surging water.

"I'll come alongside and give you a hand," called Jake knowing it was the best way to preserve his paintwork.

"Okay but hurry up," said Jess urgently. "It's hard to hold. If I let go we'll swing out fast."

By now Fin was kneeling on the wet rock helping to hold the longboat, waiting for his older brother to get in and help. "Chuck me a stern-rope. If I put some stones on it, it'll stop the dinghy

Black Jake's 'jetty'

21

swinging," he called.

"It's a longboat now," corrected Jake, but his brother and sister both ignored him and he realised it was pointless being too piratical in these circumstances. With both ends secured, the big dinghy became easier to manage and Jess passed up the first sleeping bag.

"Gimme your mobile and I'll take a picture," said Fin.

"Okay. It'll look awesome with both boats all loaded with camp gear."

"Watch out for snakes," warned Jake.

"There aren't s'posed to be any here now," replied Jess. "Not enough fresh water probably."

Fin took two pictures, one from close up and one from the bushes looking down. With *Sea Fever* in the background, this really looked like a proper expedition. Meanwhile Jess had clambered out and was taking bags from Jake.

"That's enough Fin," she called. "Hurry up and give us a hand here. We need to keep our sleeping bags off the wet rocks."

Last out were the three water containers. They were heavy and awkward, and after one had nearly dropped into the water Jake suggested tying a rope through the handle to make it easier for Jess to haul up onto the rocks. "I've got some short ropes in the top of my pack," he said to Fin. "Grab one as quick as you can!"

With the big dinghy finally empty they set up a chain gang to pass the remaining items from *Privateer*, first to the dinghy then to the rock slab. Already the tide had begun to rise and it was slightly easier to pass things up.

"We should give this landing place a name," suggested Jake. "I reckon Black Jake's Jetty."

"Yeah right! Only if we can name some other places after ourselves!" retorted Fin rather indignantly.

"Course! Now let's get this pile up in the trees. Then we can find a campsite."

"What about the boats?" reminded Jess. "The tide's rising already."

"Well, what say we lift *Privateer* above the high tide mark," suggested Jake. "Then we can drag the longboat out and use the low end of my jetty like a launching ramp later when we get Mum and Dad."

It seemed like a good idea, though by the time the boats had been rearranged safely Fin had already gone off exploring along a trail to the south. Shortly afterwards Jess headed along another worn track in the opposite direction. Meanwhile Jake tied his painter to a tree and ruefully examined the first scratches in his black paint.

It was not a particularly big island, only about three hundred metres long and two hundred wide. But being largely covered with trees and bushes, it took time to explore. Jake decided to stay near the pile of camp gear in case of native attacks, and so he could call to the others if they couldn't find their way back. Sure enough after a ten minute wait he heard Fin's call.

"Where are you?"

"Over here."

Fin pushed his way through the bushes, too pleased with himself to wait until he had even reached Jake before announcing his find. "There's a cool flat spot up near the middle. There's a big ring of stones and ashes and some logs for seats. And it's quite a grassy clearing so it'll be easy putting tents up."

They could hear Jess jogging back along her northern track. "It's not too scrubby at that end," she reported once she had caught her breath, "but it just slopes down to the sea and there's nowhere really flat for the tents. There's an old hut but it's disgusting inside. I found a bit of map too ..."

"I've found a good spot already," butted in Fin. "Come on – follow me!" From his description it seemed worthwhile to carry a first load with them, so with packs on their backs and bags in each hand they followed Fin to his campsite. Certainly it was as good a site as any they had used before, probably better than most. Jake noted with a little disappointment that it had been used as a picnic campfire by many earlier parties, but at least the island was their own for now.

"Probably a bunch of castaways were here until they were eaten by a tribe of passing cannibals," he suggested. "Anyway it's ours now and we can defend it to the death! I brought the machete to fend off invading savages."

"Stop raving on," warned Jess. "We don't want Fin having nightmares."

"I'm not a baby," retorted Fin. "Anyway there aren't any savages. What I want now is a good rock to fish from."

"Not now you don't," replied Jess sharply. "Not until we've got the camp set up decently. It has to look really good when Mum and Dad come to see it."

It took quite a lot of energy to carry the remaining loads of gear and stores to their new site. Jess estimated it was about eighty metres from Jake's Jetty, and the water containers were awkward and heavy. After struggling a few metres with the first one, Jake remembered seeing pictures of pirates carrying barrels lashed to poles.

"Wait a moment," he said and disappeared off into the scrub, returning with a dead branch. "Let's tie the handle to the middle of this pole. Then we can carry an end each." It was so much easier sharing the load, and they stopped to pose for another picture on Jess's mobile.

One of their biggest disappointments was that they wouldn't be able to use the fireplace.

"Other people have," argued Fin.

"There's a total fire ban." snapped Jess. "You know that – we've talked about it enough before. That fireplace would've been used in winter when the ground was wetter."

"Or by yobbos who don't care if they burn the island!" added Jake. "That's why we've got Jess's cooker."

The tents went up quickly, after a minor argument about their best positions. Jake wanted the two dome tents to face each other across the fireplace but Jess disagreed.

"The fireplace isn't any use really. We can't use it for anything with all those ashes in it. We might as well put the tents away a bit, facing the east so we can get morning sun into the entrances. And we can drag those logs over for seats and a sort of table."

The third tent, an old-fashioned triangular pup tent with no groundsheet, was the source of some more disagreement. Jess wanted it to be used as a toilet tent with the camp toilet inside. But Jake wanted to dig a hole for a toilet in the bushes to the south, and Fin supported him. Eventually Jess put her foot down.

"It's all very well for you guys," she said. "I like my privacy when I'm on the toilet and I haven't carted that stinkapotty all the way here for nothing. What say some savages come snooping around when we're having a bog? We can pitch it over there away from the other tents. Anyway Jake, I bet the ground's much too hard to dig a deep hole with that little shovel of yours."

Jake and Fin knew better than to argue with Jess about girls' stuff, and Jake knew she was probably right about the ground. It looked like hard clay full of rocks. Instead he and Fin set off to search for a driftwood plank for the table while Jess unloaded food supplies into her tent.

THEIR PARENTS WERE impressed when they were finally ferried ashore for an invitation cup of tea. A large black flag hung limply from a long pole near the tents, enough white patches peeking out from its folds to reveal a skull and some bones.

Jake and Fin had found two weathered grey planks washed up among the rocks on the west side and had made quite a good table by laying them across some old chunks of firewood. Jess had made a stand for her cooker out of two large rocks and some driftwood. Jake had rigged his blue tarpaulin over the main cooking area using long ropes into the surrounding trees and a couple of poles. The campsite had three long log seats around it, with skid marks showing how much effort had been needed to re-position them.

"It nearly killed us dragging them over here," commented Jake. "We used one of my ropes as a tow-rope and all pulled together."

"Well it looks great, it really does!" commented their mother. "And this is a great cuppa thanks."

"If we get a strong westerly later in the week you might need to watch that branch over the toilet tent," commented their father. "It looks a bit dodgy and you wouldn't want to be in there if it comes down on top. Otherwise you've all done a great job."

"Yeah, see what you mean Dad," said Jake. "We might shift it tomorrow. I didn't notice that."

"Okay then you lucky castaways," said their mother. "We'll row the dinghy back and keep it tonight. You've got *Privateer* if you need to get out to us."

"Okay Mum, but from now on it's the ship's longboat.

Remember that. And *Privateer* is the jollyboat when she's in rowing mode." Jake knew that if he reminded everyone often enough, they would get used to talking in proper piratical terminology.

"Sounds fine to us," said their father. "Now that we've got a whole fleet we need to tell them apart easily. Sleep well and we'll see you sometime tomorrow."

"Yes but we'll come to you, remember! Unless we fly the red signal flag. This island's out of bounds to adults except by special invitation as fellow pirates."

"Or foreign navies. Allies of course," added Jess.

It was becoming dark as their parents rowed away. Darkness falls late in the Tasmanian summer, and Jess noticed with surprise that it was after nine-thirty already. Any thoughts of the scrap of map she had picked up earlier had completely slipped her mind. Knowing from experience how hard it would be to sleep on the first night in a tent again, the three weary adventurers stowed the remaining food into Jess's tent, cleaned their teeth in seawater and crawled into their sleeping bags for a fitful night's sleep.

Chapter 4

Two Bombshells

JAKE VAGUELY HEARD FIN WRIGGLE out of the tent shortly after first light but was too tired to wake up properly. It was only when he heard the cooker hissing and Jess banging a pot that he made the effort to crawl out into the bright sunlight.

"Where's Fin?" he asked and could tell from Jess's reaction that she had thought he was still in bed.

"I hope he hasn't gone off and drowned," she exclaimed darkly. "We'd better make some camp rules about going off without telling anyone."

By the time Jake had used the toilet tent and washed in seawater, Fin cruised smugly into camp holding up three reasonable sized fish, all flathead. "I put two tiddlers back," he added. "These ones are all legal. I measured them."

Flathead

"That's good, but you can't just go off without telling anyone," said Jess crossly.

"How could I when you were all asleep? I've found a perfect spot for fishing. It's a rock near the start of the reef. I've been fishing for ages. I lost two hooks on snags but I've got plenty more. Gee I'm hungry. What's for breakfast?"

Fin was gabbling excitedly. This was his idea of a perfect holiday. He would keep the camp supplied with food for the whole week if he could fish all day. Jess was feeling more practical though.

"Cornflakes and toast for breakfast. We can cook up the fish for lunch. D'you want hot chocolate or juice? And I mean it about telling us what you're doing. We all should, so at least we know where to look for each other. Also we should wear shoes when we're away from the tents."

As she spoke there was a crackle of broken twigs and as they all turned to look, their parents walked into the clearing. "Hey you've broken our rules," called Jake. "At least you should be carrying a white flag. This is an adult-fr …" He broke off. One look at their serious faces and he knew something was wrong.

"It's Grandma," said their father, "She's in hospital. Suspected heart attack. We've got to go back to Hobart."

It was as if a bomb had gone off. A hundred thoughts flooded the campsite. Grandma not at the boat launching. Grandma and all her sailing stories. The best holiday ever – barely started and now cut short – just like that. There was a long silence.

"But …" from Fin.

"How bad is she?" That was Jake. He loved grandma dearly but he knew she would absolutely die rather than ruin such a perfect holiday.

"Do we all need to go back?" Jess was voicing what they all felt but didn't feel they could say.

"I talked to her on the hospital phone this morning," said

their mother. She's had serious chest pains and has been admitted for observation. She did say that she didn't want to spoil your camp. In fact she added a few 'shiver me timbers' and 'don't be galoots' comments – you know what grandma's like. But I really have to see her. I'd never forgive myself if …"

She didn't need to finish. It wasn't often that Mum looked so terrible.

"If it's only tests, then why doesn't Dad drop you in Kettering and we can stay on unless she gets worse," suggested Jake. "After all, she really wouldn't like to ruin a good island camping holiday."

"No! Sorry. We can't just go off and leave you kids by yourselves," replied their father.

"Why not though?" asked Jess. "It doesn't take *Sea Fever* long to get to Kettering and back. You could even go to Hobart, see Grandma and get back by mid-afternoon. And if Grandma gets worse you could phone us so we can pack up and be ready for you to pick us up. We could keep both dinghies …"

"Jollyboat and longboat," interrupted Jake.

"… so you won't have to bother about keeping them out of the way when you tie up at the marina," finished Jess.

Their parents looked at each other uncertainly. Neither was prepared to answer in the face of such a reaction.

"Give us a moment to talk about it," said their father hesitantly. The earnest way their parents were talking as they moved away towards the shoreline gave the three children a glimmer of hope.

"Honestly I absolutely know Grandma wouldn't want to spoil this camp," said Jake to the other two.

"But what if she dies and we haven't said goodbye?" said Fin.

"Perhaps we could talk to her on the hospital phone and see what she says," suggested Jess.

Jess tried hard to read her parents' faces as they returned.

She had been thinking hard too. "Do you think we could talk to Grandma by phone from here in the camp? We really do love her and it might be too late by the time we pack up if she's worse than we thought."

Her mother looked hard at all three young faces. Pulling her mobile uncertainly from her pocket, she scrolled to the dialled numbers menu and hesitated. "It's not very sensible to pester a sick person with phone calls," she murmured. "Still, I'll try and see if the nurse will put her on."

There was a long delay while she was directed to the right ward. After a short explanation to a nurse and another long pause, Grandma came on. Their mother punched the speaker-phone button so everyone could hear. Grandma sounded tired but there was a spark of excitement in her voice still.

"Are you all on Snake Island?" she asked. "How amazing this modern technology is! In my day it was flag signals and morse code. And pigeons sometimes ..." She tailed off.

"Can I speak?" asked Jess with her hand out for the phone. Her mother passed it without a word.

"It's me Grandma, Jess. We want to hear you talking. We want to tell you how much we really do love you even if we're not with you in the hospital."

"But you're exactly where I want you to be – you must know that!" came Grandma's tired but determined voice.

Jess passed the phone to Jake.

"Grandma it's Jake. I just wanted to tell you that we owe it to you that we're here right now. It's something you've given to us, with all your stories and ideas and encouragement and ..." He broke off, almost in tears and not knowing if he had quite expressed how much she had helped to form the person he had become.

"Barbecued billygoats, I'm not dying! I'm only here for tests! I feel much better today with the pills they've given me.

31

But thank you anyway, Jake. What you just said really means a lot to me."

She was starting to sound more like the lively old grandma he had known since she arrived from England nine years ago. He passed the phone to Fin.

"Hi Grandma, I caught five flathead this morning but I threw two tiddlers back, this is the coolest campsite ever, we've got three tents and made the whole island an adult-free zone except this morning when Mum and Dad came to tell us we have to go back …"

Grandma seized the pause to speak. "That's great, Fin. But can I speak to your mother now please?"

As her daughter began to speak, Grandma broke in. "Thunder and lightning, Rose! How could you even think of spoiling an expedition like this, just because I have a few chest pains!"

"Well … actually we've decided to let the children stay here for the moment," replied their mother. "Jim will run me back to Kettering in the boat so I can be with you. Then we'll see how things go. I'll be with you in a few hours. Don't do anything silly till I get there, will you. And is there anything you need from home that I can bring?"

While their mother made a list of Grandma's special little extras, the three children and their father looked at each other. It seemed like hours had elapsed since the news had broken, not a mere ten minutes. Across the water a shining cuckoo gave its distinct call and a kookaburra laughed long and loud. A crisis had been averted. Grandma had spoken. Everything seemed all right again.

HALF AN HOUR later, three truly marooned sailors watched their last link with civilisation motor away around the post that marked the end of the reef, half a kilometre to the south. Well, not quite their last link, Jess corrected herself. After all they still had her mobile as well as two boats capable of reaching the shore. But it was close enough to being truly marooned, even though Dad was going to be back by mid-afternoon.

After finishing their disturbed breakfast and cleaning up camp, they set about beginning their long planned explorations, each with a different goal in mind. Jake had for weeks been dreaming about buried treasure. It wasn't such a silly idea, he figured. He had read months ago about a sailing ship, the *Hope*, which was wrecked to the north of Bruny Island in 1822. A fortune's worth of gold coins had been salvaged from the wreck and supposedly buried on Nebraska beach only a few kilometres north of Snake Island. It had never been found, and there was no reason why it might not have been re-buried here on this very island. In fact he had almost convinced himself that this was the most likely place, being the closest small island, especially after seeing that red-bearded kayaker and his suspicious looking map here last year. Jake's goal for the day was to take his shovel and seek out the most likely spots for buried treasure, assuming that the ground would still have the same hard and soft places as it had nearly two hundred years ago.

MEANWHILE JESS HAD her mind set on mapmaking. A few weeks earlier she had looked up Snake Island on Google Earth to make an outline, but then she had decided it would be cheating so now she was going to start from scratch. She had only an orienteering compass but it would be good enough to make a series of lines to start. She knew that the magnetic variation was fifteen degrees east so she could map it first and adjust it to true north afterwards. Dad had lent her his fifty metre tape-measure so she could put in a series of markers to check the distance along her transect lines.

She pulled out the scrap of waterstained map she had picked up yesterday and squinted at it. A couple of red crosses showed near a curving shoreline but there were no features to show where it might be on the island – if in fact it was even on this island. Certainly it had been folded many times and this segment had come away from a larger photocopied map. "Jake might be interested in this," she thought, before driving in the first transect peg.

FIN, NOT SURPRISINGLY, was on the hunt for fish. Not just flathead, but bigger specimens like snapper or escaped salmon. He had brought two hand-lines and two rods, and the best hand-line had a fifteen kilogram breaking-strain nylon line. Using the biggest fish head from this morning's efforts he baited up the strong hand-line, and threw it as far out as he could. Then he did the same with a rod. Satisfied that he had a good chance, he secured them the best way he could and waited.

Three incidents spoiled what should have been a perfect day. The first was a minor invasion. A pair of peace-seeking sea kayakers strayed unknowingly into their adult free zone, landing on the north-eastern shore for a snack and some solitude. They left in less than half an hour, somewhat dismayed by the noise of what seemed like a huge tribe of kids yelling at each other and playing noisily in the scrub nearby.

"We could call them seals, like Grandma used to," suggested Jake as the three rather guilty young culprits watched them paddle away. "I guess we can't stop a few seals from hauling out on our island. But anyway it's good to know we can put them off so easily!"

The second invasion was not so easy to dismiss and was to cast a more significant shadow over the happy band of castaways. But before it occurred, another bombshell was dropped which changed their status into more genuine castaways.

IT WAS AFTER lunchtime when Jess took the phone-call on her mobile. It was from Dad and he wasn't happy at all.

"Sorry Jess, but I've been really stupid. I guess I'm more dependent on you three kids as crew than I realised."

"Why Dad, what's happened? How's Grandma?"

"Mum's with Grandma already," replied her father. "The doctor thinks she has angina, and that it wasn't a heart attack, which is good news. Angina can be treated with pills, so she might be out in a few days after more tests. But I've got a problem here. I fouled the stern-line around the propeller when I left the jetty to come back and it seems to have damaged the shaft bearing. I'm going to have to haul the boat out on the slip tomorrow to fix it, and I can't sail back over today without any wind. So stupid of me!"

"Don't worry Dad. We're fine here. Really we are. It makes it a better adventure being truly marooned."

"I can always get Doug to come over and rescue you in his runabout. He could probably be there in a couple of hours."

Jess was horrified at the thought. "Honestly Dad we absolutely positively don't need rescuing. But if it makes you happy I promise we'll ring for rescue if anything goes wrong."

"Well ... are you really sure you can cope? What about the others ...? Will they be alright? Especially Fin. You know what

I mean – he's not as old as you other two."

"Yeah Dad, stop stressing! They're having a ball. It's so cool here. I'll bet not many other kids get the chance to camp like this on their own deserted island. Just go and fix the prop and relax. We're fine."

"Well ... if you're really sure ... but you'll have to keep your mobile on so we can stay in touch. And make sure you ring me if there's any problem at all."

Jess felt a surge of relief. "Thanks heaps Dad!! Love you. See you tomorrow."

"You will take care, won't you Jess? I suppose it's only one night, after all. See you tomorrow then. Be careful ... Bye for now."

As she pushed the red button on her phone, Jess looked at the battery indicator. Just under half. Perhaps she should talk less and text more, she thought, as she called her brothers to tell them the latest news.

Chapter 5

Unwelcome Seals

FIN WAS STILL WAITING FOR his big fish. He had set the reel on low tension with a clicker on so it would scream if it had a big strike. The handline had a tin can tied to it, balanced on a branch so it would fall off in a strike making enough noise to alert him. Meanwhile he was casting a small spinner with his other rod near where the reef ran out to the south. Nothing much was happening, and he decided that slack low water at around five o'clock would be his best chance.

He had picked up Jess's mobile from the camp table after lunch, and decided to mind it for her until she noticed that she didn't have it. Meanwhile he was enjoying playing pinball on the games menu to pass the time.

The engine noise from an outboard motor caught his attention, and he idly watched a large aluminium runabout skimming fast across Great Bay, curving towards the island. As it approached he could make out two people, and it became obvious they were going to land somewhere near the opposite end of the island. He considered leaving his lines to have a look, but just then his tin fell off and he busied himself pulling it in and replacing the sadly nibbled fish-head bait with his last head. Then he decided to break off a few oysters from the rocks and throw them out near the bait as a tempting treat for a fat snapper. It was some time before he remembered the aluminium boat.

JAKE HAD DECIDED to try a circumnavigation of the island in *Privateer* for the afternoon as a change from treasure hunting. There was only a very light north-easterly breeze today, but it would be fine in his new pirate ship and he knew his parents wouldn't mind him sailing in such safe weather.

He was halfway along the eastern shore heading south towards the reef when he heard the outboard. More seals, he grumbled to himself, but was reluctant to come ashore anywhere that might damage his paint. So he continued his clockwise circumnavigation, noticing Fin playing with a fishing line and waving as he sailed past.

It was not until he had sailed through the shallow reef area and started his way north along the western side of the island that he noticed smoke curling from the far end. Alarmed, he called to Fin not knowing that his younger brother was making too much noise breaking oysters off the rocks.

If only there was a better sailing breeze, he thought, regretting that he had left the oars back at Jake's Jetty.

JESS WAS HALFWAY along an east-west transect line when she heard the outboard slow down and die. Drat, she thought to herself, and continued the compass line and tape measure work. If she stopped now she would never find her pegs, so it was a while before she completed measuring the width of the island.

She didn't see the smoke, she smelled it, and as soon as she had recorded the last part of her line she hid the compass and tape and ran off towards the source.

There were two men in black tee-shirts, one quite fat. Too fat for a seal, more like an elephant-seal, she thought to herself. Their boat was a rather battered tinny with some horrible anti-Green stickers on its sides. They had lit an enormous fire in a stone fireplace near the trees. Jess was alarmed.

The men were laughing and drinking beer. Even as Jess watched, one of them threw an empty beer-bottle towards the fire where it smashed on a stone. She fought against an impulse to walk up and demand that they put the fire out before they set the whole island alight. As she hesitated she became more and more worked up. "If only the world wasn't so full of stupid yobbos who don't care," she thought.

Without thinking of her own situation, Jess couldn't stop herself from striding out of the trees towards the fire. She was really angry now, but had still not worked out what to say first when she was noticed by the fat one.

"Take a look there Col," he said loudly to his mate. "Hey luv, what's your name?"

Jess opened her mouth to speak but the fat one spoke first. "All by yourself on the island are you? I didn't see any boats. And you are a pretty thing aren't you!" He started walking towards her.

Jess's anger was turning rapidly to alarm. She started to speak but her voice seemed so quiet compared to his. "Don't you know there's a fire ban?" she said, far too meekly.

The fat man kept advancing. There was a glint in his eye and he spoke more softly now while the other one just stood, watching. Both seemed to be staring at her tee-shirt and she blushed with embarrassment.

"Have you got a bikini under that?" asked the man. "Tell you what – I'm a famous photographer and I'll pay you to pose for me. It's quite legal now. How does twenty bucks sound?"

At this distance Jess could see he was sweating and licking his lips rather nervously. The other one laughed, a short harsh laugh, and leered at her. It was as if she was glued to the ground. Overcome with shame and humiliation, Jess simply did not know what she should do or say, and the man advanced even closer. Suddenly there was a yell from the trees, a high pitched voice that could only be Fin's. She swung round to see him pointing her phone camera towards the men.

"Mum, Dad, come quickly," he was calling out. "Some stupid men are going to burn the island down!"

It was as if he had broken a spell. Jess became unglued and ran towards him. The men talked briefly to each other and hurried back to their boat. In a couple of moments they were off, nearly upsetting *Privateer* in their wake as they roared past Jake.

"Gee Fin, lucky you came," she said, shaking slightly. "It got them worried when you pretended Mum and Dad were here! Pretending to take a picture helped get rid of them too." Fin had gone up several notches in her respect for him.

"Dunno really." He shrugged. "I just thought it might put them off. It looked like the fat one was hassling you. And I did take a picture."

The conversation ended abruptly with a shout from Jake. He had taken out his centreboard and was using it as a paddle, heading straight in to the stony shallows with little regard for the damage the sharp rock oysters would do to his paintwork.

"The fire!" he was yelling. "Do something!"

Sparks had landed among the dry grass around the crude ring of stones the men had used for a fireplace. Even as they looked the flames spread further.

"Grab the bucket from the longboat Fin," yelled Jess, running towards the spreading flames and stamping as hard as she could. Jake was racing toward her with a bailer full of seawater. He threw it into the fireplace, and with a hiss and several spitting noises the fire died down quite noticeably. Jake was panting – it had been hard work paddling in and running.

"Get another bailer full," he puffed to Jess. "I'll stay and stamp." He threw his lifejacket as far from the fire as he could and jumped onto the burning tufts of grass. At least the ground here was fairly bare, but he knew if the flames reached the thicker dry grass higher up the slope, there would be no stopping them. Jess was already hurrying back with more water, and in the distance behind her he could see a wooden dinghy being rowed fast and steady towards them across the water from an old house in Snake Bay.

Fin's bucket probably saved the day. And Jake was now grateful that the wind was so light. They were standing around the blackened circle of ground when the varnished clinker dinghy Jake had noticed scrunched up onto the gravel beach and a grey haired man climbed out. He looked furious, striding towards them with surprising speed for his apparent age.

"You young fools!" he exclaimed angrily. "Don't you know there's a fire ban? You can't just waltz onto this island lighting fires. This place is far too special."

"But we didn't ..." Jess started to explain.

"Not knowing is no excuse," the man interrupted, still angry. "We've been trying to ban camping here because of idiots like you. And where are your parents? I'd like to speak to them."

"They're not here," said Jake lamely, knowing it sounded bad. "They've gone back to Kettering."

Mumbling about irresponsible parenting, the man turned his back and looked at the charred circle. They noticed he had a hearing aid.

"And don't you know you can't keep undersized fish!" he

exclaimed, pointing at a pile of five flathead lying near the fire – obviously intended for the black-shirted men's lunch. Even Jake could see that three of the fish were too small.

"They aren't m…" began Fin indignantly, but the man was either unable or unwilling to listen.

"Of course they are. I'll be watching you," he concluded, still angry. "That's my shack over there and I can see what goes on through my binoculars. I'd only just arrived when I saw your smoke, but next time you go lighting fires I'll be calling the fire service."

He stumped away. Jake couldn't help admiring his lovely old dinghy and the ease with which he rowed it. "Pity about the owner," he thought to himself. They were silent. It was as if a dark cloud had descended over their piece of paradise.

Jess hardly spoke at all on the way back to camp after they had carried *Privateer* up into the trees for Jake to de-rig and examine the new scratches. It was all too much, she thought. How am I going to cope in the navy if I can't stand up to a couple of stupid yobbos and a deaf old man? She almost gave in to the temptation to ring her father, or maybe even talk to Vanessa – her best friend – to talk about the incidents. Looking at her mobile she noticed with a shock that the battery was now down to its last quarter.

"The battery's down. You haven't been ringing your friends on this have you?" she asked Fin. "And how come you had it anyway?"

"You left it at the camp so I was minding it," he answered, wondering how much battery his pinball games had used. "I haven't rung anybody, you can check."

Jess was thinking it was probably a good thing that Vanessa and most of her other friends were away on holiday. She had told them she would be camping out of range. Just as well nobody had rung her anyway, or her battery would be already flat.

Fin wandered off to check his lines. He was feeling frustrated and small. How could that old man accuse them of lighting fires and catching undersized fish? Especially the fish – Fin had always been careful to measure his catch and put the tiddlers back carefully so they would survive. He hated being told off by his teachers and this was even worse. That man might even complain to the police. He began to wish Dad was back.

His long fishing rod was still there, the nylon line hanging loosely to the water's edge. But the tin can had fallen off the branch where he had tied the strong handline, and he noticed that most of the extra line which he had left loose on the ground had disappeared. With a little shiver of expectation he hurried out onto the big rocky outcrop and began to pull it in. At first he thought there was nothing on, but suddenly with a shock he felt the strain come on. It was heavy, very heavy. In fact he didn't know if he could hold it any longer.

Fin had cut his hands before on a handline, so he knew what would happen if he let it slide through his fingers. There was nothing to do except let go and watch the line pull steadily away until it slowed and reached as far as its length would allow. Fin expected the line to break, but the knot held. Perhaps the fish or shark or whatever it was had been swimming at an angle and was being pulled around in a circle like a dog on a leash. He yelled shrilly to Jess for help.

Not that there was much Jess could do, but it took her mind off her self-doubts. She took in the situation as soon as she arrived and was back to her old self again.

"Wrap your shirt around your hands," she said. "I will too." Lucky she had a bikini top under, she thought, briefly thinking of the greasy fat man before erasing him from her thoughts.

Together they grasped the line and began pulling steadily. At first it was just a heavy line but as it drew closer to the shore they began to feel the power of whatever the monster was that Fin

"Something big on, really big!"

had hooked. It didn't feel like an ordinary fish which would pull fiercely in short bursts. No, this was a heavy almost lazy power which simply didn't give up.

"I can see something!" yelled Fin excitedly, noticing a large dark patch in the water, the size of a small table.

"What's happening?" Jake had arrived now, attracted by their excited voices.

"Something big on, really big!" Fin was beside himself with excitement.

"It's a stingray, a big one!" Jess had been the first to recognise what the big wide black patch was that they were hauling in.

They gasped, almost as a single combined gasp, each thinking of the danger and achievement of catching such a monster. As it approached the rocks the big ray seemed to double its power. It was trying to turn away but was having difficulty turning while they pulled it towards them.

"Take a picture Jake. The mobile's in my pocket." Jess knew

they would have to cut it loose. It would be far too dangerous to land it with its evil barb of poison lashing behind it. Anyway it was against their principles to kill something they couldn't eat. But a photo would be enough.

"Wait till it rises to the surface. That's it. Now." It was as if the horrible experiences of the afternoon were being covered over with a big blanket. Jess was back to herself again. She would cope in the navy. She could give commands. She knew how to respond to emergencies.

"Right, where's your knife, Fin?"

"But ..." Fin could hardly bear the thought of cutting away the biggest fish he had ever seen, but he knew Jess was right. Reaching as far as he could, to save as much precious nylon as he could, Fin sliced through the line. The giant ray hesitated, nearly on the surface, its baleful pair of eyes seeming to glare at them. They watched spellbound as it gracefully turned and glided down, away from the island into the deep.

Chapter 6

Foreign Allies

IT HAD BEEN A STRESSFUL DAY with so many ups and downs. Jess didn't think she had ever experienced such a day. It seemed like a week already since they had set up camp, not just twenty-four hours.

They were sitting around the campsite, eating dinner and discussing the afternoon invaders. Jess felt better about it all now, especially as she knew in her heart that she had done nothing wrong and truly had helped prevent a disaster. One day even that deaf old man would know the truth, she was sure.

"We should call that grouchy old man Captain Bligh," she announced. "He thinks he owns this island, but he doesn't." Somehow she found that giving him a nickname brought him back down to size.

Jake had helped her cook macaroni cheese. They had eaten fish for lunch so they had decided there was no need to open any canned stew. Fin had managed to make a chocolate instant dessert using milkpowder without too many lumps. He had added some chopped up dates to make them eat it more slowly.

"Did you see if there was a rego number on their boat?" Jake asked between mouthfuls. He had been far too busy trying not to capsize when they raced past him to notice any details.

"No, but it had a Johnson outboard and stickers on its side. 'Greens Tell Lies' and 'Kill Ferals'," she replied.

"What's a feral?" asked Fin.

"Really it means animals turned wild, like wild cats or dogs," answered Jake. "But I think the sticker means people who've become hippies – you know, gone to live in the wild and look after the trees."

"Yeah – not burn them down like those ignorant black-shirts," added Jess, still angry at the nerve of those horrible men. As they finished eating Fin's chocolate dessert they became aware of the deep rumble of a diesel engine, followed by the unmistakable clanking of anchor chain. Torn between dismay and curiosity all three children leapt to their feet. "Don't let anyone see us," said Jess. "They might be a hostile navy."

"Or an enemy pirate flagship," added Jake. Quietly in the

"It's the Kiwi boat."

dimming evening light, they made their way to Jake's Jetty. The longboat was still there, dragged up above the high tide mark at the edge of the trees.

"P'raps they'll think it's an old abandoned dinghy," whispered Fin.

"That's the Kiwi schooner we saw in Kettering," said Jess in low tones.

"It's a ketch, not a schooner," Jake corrected. "See how the front mast is bigger than the back one. Pity – a schooner would be more like a pirate ship. I reckon it's at least twelve metres long."

"There are kids on board. I saw them," whispered Fin. Sure enough, across the water came the unmistakable chatter of children's voices. A girl laughed and a slightly deeper voice was talking about fishing. Then a man said something about food and they made out shapes of people walking back from the bow and disappearing into the cabin.

As they returned to camp, Jess felt a shiver of hopeful anticipation pass through her body. Despite her pleasure at having an island to themselves, she wouldn't mind so very much having some other kids to meet. Especially ones who had sailed all the way from another country. Her brothers obviously didn't feel quite the same curiosity.

"They'd better not catch all my fish," grumbled Fin.

"They probably think they're the world's best sailors," agreed Jake. Jess kept her feelings to herself.

They were really tired this evening. The hard ground had not given them a comfortable night's rest last night. They watched some tiny birds flittering like butterflies through the branches of the big trees around the campsite for a while, but soon found themselves all yawning. Before they crawled into bed Jess sent her father a text:

Hi dad hope alls fine for u. We r still fine. Battery low so will
only text now on. Will switch off at night. Love to mum & gma
- jj&f

The urge she had felt earlier, to tell her father all about the
day's horrible events, had vanished.

She fell asleep, dreaming of meeting a handsome young
Kiwi sailor.

FIN DIDN'T BEAT them out of bed next morning. In fact he
was the last up. The first thing he did was ask Jess to show him
the stingray photo on her mobile. As soon as she switched it on,
a text message came up :

Hi u castaways. Grandma getting better. Mum will stay 4 now.
Sf goes on slip at 11. Hope for quick fix. C u tonite take care
love dad.

She read it aloud to Fin and Jake. The photo wasn't too bad
really – the stingray showed up as a black triangle with its long
lethal tail trailing a long way behind.

"It'll look better blown up on a computer screen," said Jake.
Fin beamed with pride.

"I'll take a big print to school," he crowed. "Can't wait for
Tom to see it. He thinks he's the best at fishing."

"Keep your voice down," warned Jake. "We don't want the
Kiwis to know we're here."

They talked it over between themselves. After the invasions
of the day before, they were feeling quite possessive of their
island. Jess didn't say much. She was happy just to let things
happen. Secretly she had a good feeling about this boatload

of possible invaders, but she didn't want to disagree with her brothers.

"If they come ashore we'll hide in the scrub and watch," Fin was saying. "If they come into the camp we could tie them up."

"Don't get too carried away," advised Jake. "We can't actually do anything much to them. But anyway if we're unfriendly enough they'll go away."

An outboard motor started up and they hurried to Stingray Rock (Fin's new name for it). Peering through the leaves they could see a grey inflatable heading out to the end of the reef. They saw enough to make out two dark-haired kids inside.

"I hate them!" said Fin. "Wish we had a boat like that. And now they're going to catch the best fish." Sure enough, as they watched, they saw two fish being reeled in and quickly thrown back. Ten minutes later the inflatable was buzzing down the west side of the island.

"I don't think they'll see *Privateer*," said Jake as they hurried down the track to the opposite end of the island. "She's hidden well up in the trees."

Peering through the scrub they watched a boy and girl nose their boat up on the gravel beach, carefully avoiding the sharp oysters. They were about Jess or Jake's age, more tanned than the Brownrig kids. The boy had a mass of black curly hair and the girl, who looked rather refined, had beautiful long black wavy hair. Jess wondered why she didn't keep it in a ponytail like her own hair.

They almost laughed when they saw how these Kiwi kids were dressed. Their jeans were tucked into long sea-boots and they were putting on coats and gloves. As they walked into the bushes the boy walked in front of the girl, banging the ground with every step. Lying flat on the ground, the three watched them slowly follow the trail towards their campsite.

"What on earth are they doing?" whispered Jess.

"Dunno. Let's dodge around past my jetty and cut'em off. They'd better not pinch any of our stuff," whispered Jake.

The pair were standing just inside the campsite clearing, looking uncertain of themselves, when the defenders sneaked up.

"Didn't think there was anyone on the island," the boy was saying.

"Better not get too close. Could be someone in a tent," said the girl.

"Look. There's some of those squashy fish heads," said the boy. "P'raps they eat them here."

As the curly-haired boy stooped to examine Fin's bait bucket, Fin couldn't resist having his say. Bursting out of the scrub, he was alongside the boy in no time. "They're flathead heads. Tiddler ones but I didn't catch them – I only catch legal ones. Some yobbos left them yesterday so I kept 'em for bait. Something ate the bodies last night. Haven't you seen flatheads before?"

The curly headed boy stepped back, not expecting such a torrent of information, or anyone at all for that matter. "We caught three much bigger ones this morning out by the reef," he replied rather shyly.

"They looked too ugly to eat, so we chucked them back," added the girl who had stepped up once she realised Fin was not a threat. "Sorry we came into your campsite. We didn't even know there was anyone on the island till now."

Jake and Jess had moved close behind as they talked. When Jess coughed they spun around, startled.

"Oh hi. I'm Zac. This is Tania. Twin sister, ay." Zac had brown eyes and a firm chin, Jess noticed. And he spoke slightly differently from how she expected. His vowels came out differently from the Australian accent she had grown up with.

"I'm Jess, this is Jake. You've already met Fin."

"My real name's Fintan but people call me Fin which is better coz fish have fins and I love fishing."

He always talks far too much when he's excited, thought Jess privately as Fin babbled on.

"And Jess is really Jacinta but we call her Jess because she doesn't like being shortened to Cindy. Jake's Jacob but he likes being Black Jake, the pirate." Fin pointed at the flag which was now fluttering more distinctly. Jake squirmed a little, wondering if they would laugh at him.

"What's Zac short for?" asked Jess shyly. "Zaccariah?"

"Nah – my real name's Anzac," responded the Kiwi boy. "Named after my grandad, Mum's dad, ay."

Jess knew about the Australian and New Zealand wartime connection, but she didn't know anyone named after an army battalion.

"It's not an uncommon name in New Zealand," added Tania.

"Aren't you hot, dressed like that?" asked Jake, breaking his silence at last.

The twins looked at the three Australian children, suddenly aware of the contrast between their coats and boots and these kids' shorts and slip-on footwear.

"Snakes," said Tania.

"And scorpions," added Zac rather self-consciously. Jess tried not to laugh.

"We don't think there's any snakes left on this island," she said. "And even if there was they'd probably be slithering away to hide when they heard you guys coming."

"That's why we were banging." said Zac. "To scare 'em off. There's no snakes in New Zealand."

"They'll hear you walking from miles away," explained Jess, not wanting them to feel too foolish. She liked them and it could be fun having them around.

"What about your feet though?" asked Tania. "Don't you wear

anything except jandals? What happens if a scorpion stings you?"

"What are jandals?" asked Jess, puzzled. "D'you mean these?" She slipped one off her right foot. "We call them thongs. We only wear them around camp usually. Except this morning we rushed off to spy on you guys." It was funny, she thought later, how two countries so close together could still have little language differences.

Fin broke in, eager to talk fishing again. "Don't you have flatheads where you come from?" he asked.

"We mostly sail near Cook Strait," replied Zac. "We keep the boat in Wellington, and sail in the Marlborough Sounds."

"That's the top of the South Island," explained Tania.

"We catch heaps of spotties but they're only good for bait. Too small ay. The best fish are blue cod and snapper."

"We get red cod here and sometimes snapper," replied Fin. "I caught a huge stingray yesterday." Zac looked impressed, but then he looked at Tania and at his watch.

"We've gotta get back now. Been too long already, ay. P'raps you can come out and see us after lunch. Where's your parents?"

"Oh, they went back to the mainland for a while," said Jake, casually. After all there was no time to explain everything and he didn't want to make his father sound too stupid. "Anyway we've made this island an adult-free zone."

"We'll give you a signal when to come," suggested Tania. "I'll hoist a red flag."

"That's our signal too," exclaimed Fin as the Kiwi kids removed their gloves and coats and began walking back to their boat. "See ya later then."

A new ANZAC alliance had begun.

Chapter 7

Good and Not-so-good News

THE MORNING SEEMED TO DRAG now there was something new to look forward to. After they had cleaned up the breakfast, Jake and Jess shifted the toilet tent away from under the rotten branch. Meanwhile Fin was finding it hard to scrub the pots and dishes from last night's dinner using seawater.

"I'll see if fresh water works better at soaking out that mess the burnt cheese made in that pot," said Jake.

"Okay but we can't afford to waste much fresh water," warned Jess. But when Jess tried to get them all to roll up their sleeping bags navy style, neither of her brothers was interested.

"I'm a pirate, not a navy sailor," argued Jake. "I should be sleeping in a hammock."

Once the camp was tidy they set about continuing their activities from the previous day. Jess headed off to measure some more lines at the north end of the island, while Fin tried fishing from a spot near Jake's Jetty where he could watch the ketch for a red flag.

Jake was off with his shovel, determined to keep trying for the buried treasure. He knew that there were a lot of coins, for soldiers' wages. Probably gold sovereigns back in 1822, he

54

thought, though maybe crowns and shillings too. Hopefully in a box and not bags. He wondered if a box would have rotted away by now. Certainly a bag would have turned to dust. If he hadn't been boatbuilding he could have afforded a metal-detector. Maybe next year he could bring one if he didn't succeed this year.

In books about treasure there was always a map to help people find it. Jake tried to remember more details of the furtive red bearded kayaker he had seen here once before. He definitely had a map and was searching around, but as far as Jake could remember there was no sign of any spade or shovel.

He decided the best plan would be to imagine he was a runaway sailor two hundred years ago, trying to find somewhere on this island where the ground was soft enough to bury a box. The ground was probably the same then except maybe some of the trees would have died and been replaced by new ones in different places. At first he tried working his way clockwise around the shoreline, prodding the ground for soft spots. After half an hour he changed his mind. The ground here seemed to be far too rocky, with just a thin layer of soil. He decided that if he was a nineteenth century coin thief, he would probably go somewhere further into the centre where nobody would see him from a boat or telescope from the shore. He soon found that the best places to dig were around the roots of fallen trees.

Before long he started worrying about the mess his digging was making. What would Captain Bligh say if he came to inspect the place and found holes everywhere? He went back over his tracks and filled in the holes neatly, covering any bare dirt with leaves and twigs. There were a few animal droppings near one hole, looking fairly fresh. Jake wondered what sort of creature would be living on the island. A possum perhaps? He hadn't seen anything wandering around in the daytime, but maybe it was a night animal. Occasionally he had seen a few lizards though. He hoped Jess was right about snakes here.

As he filled in his holes, it occurred to him that the tree roots which made these softer spots would almost certainly have been the roots of tall standing trees back in the days when any loot was buried. This treasure hunting was not as easy as he first thought! What if a new tree had grown where the original hole was dug. There might be treasure right underneath one of the very trees he was looking at now. He wondered how old these big gum trees would be before they died and fell down. Besides, the coins may not even have been buried on this island anyway. Or they might have been secretly dug up and spent a hundred years ago.

Already Jake was getting tired of digging. The shovel was too small to dig properly, and the day was getting hot. He wandered off to find Fin.

"I got another flathead," called his younger brother as soon as he heard Jake approaching. "But I lost two more hooks on snags. I'm trying to catch a salmon on my spinner. No luck yet."

"Any sign of life on the ketch yet?" asked Jake. He squinted at the two masts looking for a red flag but only the tiny Australian flag fluttered at the spreaders. "I'm gonna rig *Privateer* for another sail. Sea-breeze might kick in soon. Can you gimme a hand to carry her down?"

Fin too had grown rather bored with his morning's activities. He was pleased to do something different. "Can I come out too? Should be safe. I'll do whatever you tell me."

Jake thought about it. There was no real danger, though he wasn't sure how happy Mum and Dad would be. At least there was another yacht around to help if they needed it. And they had a rescue boat of their own too. "Okay, but we'll get the longboat ready so Jess can come out if we need help."

It was nearly high tide as they slid the longboat to a position where Jess would be able to push off by herself. After tying the painter to a tree they set off to find Jess.

She was banging a peg into the ground when they found her, not far from where *Privateer* was hidden. "Have they hoisted their red flag already?" she asked eagerly. "It's not even lunch time."

"Nah but we're gonna take *Privateer* for a sail now," announced Fin cockily, waiting for a reaction from his bossy sister. Surprisingly she didn't seem against the idea.

"Guess it's safe enough for you both. Can't see Mum and Dad minding you going with Jake in these conditions. You'll need your lifejacket though. Hey Jake do you think I could come out after him?" She could picture herself and Jake sailing past the white ketch, and could almost imagine Zac watching her enviously.

"Okay – as long as the sea-breeze doesn't get too strong. We've dragged the longboat down so you can push it in by yourself. Just in case we need a hand. Pity we can't leave it moored in the water all day."

Jake rigged the mast and sail while Fin ran back for lifejackets and sea boots. Jake was insisting they wore things on their feet that would protect them from the razor-sharp oysters. Jess helped them carry *Privateer* down the gravel northern beach to the water.

"If we put her in with the stern out I should be able to rig the rudder," said Jake. "Then Fin can hop in the bow and if you give her a shove Jess, I think I can sail her backwards into deeper water. Fin you'll be in charge of the centreboard. Use it as a paddle till I say, then push it half down."

Jake was pleased that last year's sailing lessons were going to be useful now. He was already more confident in *Privateer* and looking forward to being a captain with crew.

"We'll sail around to my jetty, Jess. Keep an eye on us. If you launch the longboat we can tie both boats there while we have lunch."

It was an enjoyable half hour for all three of them. Jess was pleased to have something different to do, and managed to push the longboat into the water without too much difficulty. It was always fun to go rowing, and she set to work heading towards where she thought Jake and Fin would be on their next tack. They were making slow progress against the light easterly headwind as they crossed the shallow stretch of water between the island and the Snake Bay shore.

"I suppose Captain Bligh is watching through his binoculars," called Fin.

"Too bad if he is," retorted Jess, resting on her oars. "There's no law against this. We're wearing our lifejackets."

There was still no red flag on the ketch as they approached Jake's Jetty. They were all starting to feel hungry, and after some talk they decided to take down *Privateer*'s mast and sail, and take the Optimist in tow. Fin could steer her while Jess and Jake rowed the longboat alongside Jake's Jetty. Then they could tie up two abreast like the first day, with enough ropes to stop them blowing onto the large rocks further in.

"If the sea-breeze gets too strong we'll have to pull them out of the water or find a spot around the other side," said Jake. "But they should be okay till after lunch if we're quick."

It was stale bread sandwiches with corned beef and tomatoes today. No-one felt like a hot drink, so after some juice and while the boys were cleaning up, Jess hurried through the trees for a look at their friends' boat. A red flag was fluttering below the Australian one. Bursting back into camp, she called to them to hurry. Back at the jetty the sea-breeze was freshening so they decided to set *Privateer* up as a jollyboat and row both boats out together.

Tania and Zac were waiting to take their lines. Their father seemed relaxed and their mother was full of warmth and friendliness. "So you're the three castaways," she said. "Zac and

Tania are quite envious of you!"

"This is Jake and Jess and Fin", said Tania. "This is Mum and Dad."

"Miriama and Mike," corrected their mother. "And how long have you been castaways?"

"Only a couple of days," answered Jake. "Dad's probably coming back this evening. We've got an H28. Mum had to go to the hospital."

"Is she all right?" asked Mike, concerned. "She didn't have an accident I hope."

"Oh no," replied Jess hurriedly. "It's just that Grandma went in with a heart problem. But she's getting better."

"Ah," said Miriama, understanding instantly. "Your parents must have great confidence in your ability to cope. Tania and Zac have been making noises about becoming castaways too since they met you."

The three looked at each other. Jess was afraid her brothers might react badly to the idea of these Kiwi twins camping on their island and spoiling their solitude, but one look at their faces showed that they felt like she did. Their new friends seemed so interesting, and having them in the camp would be more fun.

"D'you mean you might let them come and camp with us?" asked Fin excitedly. "That'd be awesome!"

Mike smiled wistfully. "We don't see why not. They could borrow an old headsail and set it up as a bivvy. Probably just for tonight though. We may be moving further down the Channel tomorrow."

"Zac tells us the island's an adult-free zone," continued Miriama in her pleasant husky voice. "But do you think if we promise not to interfere we might be allowed to visit your camp later? Just for a sticky beak. Then we'll leave you alone."

"Of course," said Jake quickly. "You can be fellow pirates just arrived from a long sea voyage and coming with a white flag to request clear passage through our waters."

Fin was looking down the hatch as they talked, and Tania realised that they would probably like a tour below. "Come on down and have a look," she offered.

It was quite a lot bigger than *Sea Fever*. There was a cabin at the stern, where their parents slept. The main cabin had a galley in it like *Sea Fever*, but was wider and longer. The tiny bathroom had a shower and toilet, though Tania said that they didn't use the shower much while they were cruising.

"Not enough fresh water for that luxury," she explained. She and Zac shared a good sized cabin near the bow with a bunk on each side. "Our feet bang together a bit where the bunks join each other. It can get pretty horrible up here when it's rough too. Sometimes we have to sleep in the main cabin when it's rough. It gets noisy too."

"What's she built of?" asked Jake.

"She's steel," replied Zac. "Home built, ay. This is our first overseas trip."

On the ceiling of the kids' forward cabin were strapped two skateboards, a bodyboard and a snowboard.

"Are they all yours, Zac?" asked Jess.

"No, one skateboard and the bodyboard are Tania's. My surfboard's down in the passageway aft. I brought my snowboard coz I heard Tasmania was cold."

"Sometimes we get snow on Mount Wellington in summer," said Jake. "It's only a twenty minute drive up there from the city."

"We try to suss out the skate parks while we're cruising," added Zac. "The Kettering one was great! Not too crowded ay. Mum calls it our PE exercise."

They moved back into the main cabin.

"I wish *Sea Fever* was this size," said Fin. "Then we could sail up the tropics and catch heaps of tuna."

"We might one day," replied Jake. "Mum and Dad are talking

about getting something bigger. You guys are so lucky!"

"So are you," responded Zac. "We would never have been allowed to camp ashore if it hadn't been for you three."

They needed to discuss how best to get ashore. Mike offered to bring Zac and Tania across in the inflatable but the five had better ideas. There was no point involving adults when they were capable of managing among themselves. After some debate they decided that Jake and Fin would go back in the jollyboat. They would convoy Jess and the Kiwi kids in the longboat with their stores and gear. It took a while to get organised, and Jake and Jess were able to have a better look over the rigging and navigation equipment. Jess was particularly interested in the radar, so Mike turned it on for her to see.

"Those rings can be used to show distance from land or ships," he explained. "See, we're 1.2 miles from the fish farm and 0.05 from the island."

"That dot must be the cardinal mark on the end of the reef!" exclaimed Jess.

"That's right. I'll turn up the gain to make it stand out better." Jess liked Mike. He seemed a natural teacher, and she doubted he got stressed about many things.

At last Tania and Zac were ready. Things got a little wet loading them into the longboat, which was pitching in the strengthened sea-breeze. "We'll need to go around to the north end to land now," stated Jake. "It'll be too rough at the jetty."

"Is there a jetty?" asked Zac.

"Not a real one, just a rock slab that Jake discovered. But it'll be too rough there till the breeze dies down," replied Jess. They waved to the ketch as they rowed away in their little convoy. A new phase of the adventure was beginning.

Half an hour later, back at camp, Jess checked her phone. She had been watching for a sail to the west but the channel was still empty.

Not good sorry. Shaft bearing needs replacing. Won't be off slip for another day. Are u still ok? Can come for u with doug. Gma getting better & wants to know how u castaways are surviving. Text soon or I will come for u with doug. Luv dad.

Without delay Jess began texting her reply.

We are fine repeat fine. Love it here. Don't, repeat don't come for us. NZ ketch here can rescue us if needed.

She hesitated before continuing. No need to say anything about having extra campers here tonight.

Lots and lots of love from the castaways

She pushed the send button and joined the others to tell them the latest news.

Chapter 8

Night Adventures

ZAC AND TANIA WERE THRILLED with the camp. Jake envied them so much for being able to sleep like pirates under a sail, that he persuaded Tania to move in to Jess's tent so that he could join Zac. He offered her his inflatable mattress as a bribe. Tania was secretly pleased, as she was still nervous of scorpions even after being assured they were no worse than a wasp sting.

"The ants are more dangerous here," said Jake, not realising that he wasn't helping her nervousness. "Bull ants are huge and their bites are painful, but jack jumpers sometimes kill people with their sting."

Seeing Tania's reaction, Jess butted in. "It's okay Tania. We haven't seen any jack jumpers near the camp. Anyway I've got an epi-pen in case of emergencies. If your tongue swells up and you can't breathe I'll give you a jab."

Jack jumper

Both Tania and Zac were staring at her, not quite sure whether she was joking. Jess seemed so matter of fact about it all.

"Look don't worry, we're alive aren't we? We've been here for days. Just relax and forget about creepy crawlies. If you can sail across the Tasman Sea then you can survive a night on Snake Island!" Jake didn't want their new friends running back to their boat with their tails between their legs.

With the help of a few large stones to keep the sides of the sail down on the ground, Zac and Jake soon had their bivvy looking like something that most marooned sailors would be proud of. Meanwhile Jess had transferred the camp stores from her tent into Fin's, using up the empty space Jake had left behind to make room for Tania. Fin was not too happy about the changes, but as he didn't want anyone thinking he was scared to sleep on his own, he stopped himself from complaining. After all, they were all close enough to talk freely while lying in their separate tents.

Once they had the camp reorganised they sat for a while, enjoying being together and sharing the adventure. It was fun comparing their experiences. Even though they were from different countries they had so much in common.

"I googled Snake Island once," said Jess. "Do you realise we're on an island off an island off an island off a big island?" They looked at her for a moment, thinking.

"I don't get it," said Fin.

"Is Australia an island or a continent?" asked Zac.

"Some books say it's the world's largest island," continued Jess. "So Tasmania's an outlying island, Bruny Island's off its coast and we're out from Bruny. It's funny really. From here Tasmania seems like the mainland."

As they talked, Zac suddenly pointed at a beautiful blue bird flitting above the ground near their log seats.

"Look at that fantail," he exclaimed. "What an amazing colour, ay! Our ones are only brown."

"It's a blue wren," explained Jess. "They're real family birds. When the mum has her first babies of the summer she goes away and leaves them with the dad so she can build a second nest for more babies. And when the first ones start to fly they come and help get food for their new baby brothers and sisters. I read that in my bird book."

"Aren't there some amazing creatures around," said Tania. "I wonder what those ones are up in that tree?" She pointed high in a gum tree at the edge of the camp. There were several tiny spotted birds scurrying along the branches like little mice. Every now and then they could be seen flittering like flying beetles among the leaves.

"Not sure what they are. Tiny aren't they? We've been calling them 'butterfly birds' the way they flick around about," said Jess. "Wish I had my bird book here."

By now it was time to think about their evening meal. "That's weird. All the water we left in that soaking pot's gone," observed Jess, and took it down to the rocks to finish scrubbing it with seawater.

Tania and Zac had brought some canned stew and canned peaches. It seemed a pity to cook two separate dinners so they all agreed to cook up a mixed meal. Mixing in two cans of baked beans with the canned stew and adding some slices of cheese made a very filling meal, especially with toast cooked on Jess's cooker.

"Wish we could have a campfire," said Zac, though he understood quickly enough why they were not prepared to take the risk. They showed him the blackened circle from yesterday's near disaster, and told him about Captain Bligh and his binoculars.

"I read somewhere that the Australian bush has explosive gases," said Tania. "In New Zealand our trees don't catch fire so easily."

After mixing the Kiwi canned peaches with some Australian

canned plums and cornflakes, they sat around on the log seats, talking as if they had always been friends. There was so much to talk about. Zac and Tania told of their ten day ocean crossing from Wellington. Jess was full of questions about how they organised their steering watches and was amazed to hear that Zac was sometimes allowed to do night watches on his own. Tania admitted that she was still nervous being on her own in the cockpit at night, but even she spent four hours a day on watch.

"We don't have to actually steer much," admitted Zac. "The self-steering does that. But we have to keep a lookout and check the sails or engine. And sometimes plot our position on the chart." Jess was impressed. She wondered how she would cope on her own in the dark.

"It seems better when there's a bright moon," added Zac. "But in the storm it was quite freaky ay!"

"Do all Kiwis talk like you – saying 'ay' all the time," asked Fin – much to Jess's embarrassment.

"No! I don't, do I?" replied Tania instantly.

"Dunno really, ay", said Zac thoughtfully. "Most of my mates do so it's just a habit I guess. Tania doesn't, coz she's a bit of a princess!"

"We've got an English girl in our class who says 'like' at the end of every sentence," added Jess, anxious to let Zac know she wasn't critical of his manner of talking.

As he spoke they heard the murmur of approaching adult voices, and soon Mike and Miriama walked into the clearing. Mike was waving a small white flag.

"We come in peace," he said solemnly. "Permission for safe passage through pirate waters?" Jess burst out laughing when she saw them clearly. Mike had painted a long scar across his left cheek and was wearing a red scarf around his head. Miriama had a gypsy style skirt and an eye patch.

"It'll cost you three gold sovereigns," replied Jake with false seriousness, and their eyes widened as Miriama pulled out a small pouch and counted out not three, but ten gold foil covered chocolate coins.

"Two each for the marooned pirates' supper," she said with a smile.

"Safe passage for ever then," declared Jake, and they took their guests for a guided tour of the camp. Tania told her parents about the creepy-crawly dangers and Mike made a show of hopping around pretending the ground was covered with ants.

Miriama was impressed with their toilet tent. "It's horrible in some campsites seeing piles of toilet paper everywhere under the bushes," she said.

While Jess made everyone a mug of hot chocolate on her cooker, they all talked. Jake told of a story he had read about Snake Island's history. There was a family – he thought there were about nine children – who lived on the island during the convict era. They had a couple of cows and grew crops. One day some escaped convicts landed on the island with a musket and axe, threatening to shoot the father unless they were given supplies. The oldest son and daughter fought them off after their father was wounded in a knife fight and later the family was granted a reward for its bravery.

"There might be some relics or bricks left from their house," said Mike thoughtfully. Jess was thinking of her own similar encounter with threatening invaders. A shiver ran down her spine at the thought of how desperate the poor mother must have felt.

Jake poured the drinks. They had only five mugs, so he used the two fruit cans for the last two and kept them for himself and Jess as hosts. But as soon as Zac noticed Jess trying to hold the scalding hot can, he insisted on swapping it for his own mug.

"I've got heat-resistant fingers, ay," he grinned, and Jess couldn't stop herself from blushing at his consideration.

It was growing dark as the two Kiwi adult pirates said their farewells and they all walked with them back to the inflatable. "Here's the hand-held, Zac," his father said, as they were about to paddle out into the water. "It's switched to channel 77. Don't turn it on unless you need to call us – that'll save the battery. We'll leave the boat VHF on all night so we'll hear if you call. Sleep well, all you castaways."

The water was as calm as a mirror, and a fingernail moon hung above the western sky. No-one wanted to go to bed, so after cleaning up the dinner mess, Fin persuaded them all to come to Stingray Rock for some night fishing. They had to share his two rods and two handlines, but none of them minded. It was good to have an excuse to stay up late. Fin was particularly thrilled to be the one giving instructions.

"Keep that line clear of the weeds over there," he told Zac. "I snagged two hooks there yesterday."

As Zac flung his hook and sinker out into clear water, a ball of brilliant blue light seemed to explode where it splashed, and rings of light spread out around it. They had all seen this bioluminescence before, but that didn't reduce the thrill of seeing it tonight. Somehow it was like watching fireworks, always a joy to see. They took turns to throw stones into the water until Fin told them it would scare away the fish. "Not that there are many fish here," he grumbled. "We should be out over the reef if we really want to catch fish."

There was a silence, as all thoughts focussed on what Fin had said. After all, it was a flat calm evening with a little moonlight.

"We could take the VHF in case we get into trouble ..." suggested Zac, voicing what they were all thinking.

"We've all got lifejackets. It would be perfectly safe ..." added Jess.

"Let's do it!" announced Jake suddenly. "We'll all fit in the longboat."

Jess noticed that Tania clutched her arm rather tightly as they threaded their way through the dark trees on their way to the longboat at the opposite end of the island, and sensed that she was shivering slightly. They were only using one torch and had agreed not to use it in the longboat unless they needed it, to avoid being seen.

"Not that we're doing anything really wrong," Jake had said, "but we don't want your parents worrying about us."

The tide was nearly in as they carried the longboat into the water. "Good," said Fin. "Best fishing's at slack water."

It was a longer row than they thought along the western side of the island out of sight of the ketch. The oars dipped into exploding balls of blue light with each stroke, and a pair of brilliant blue lines peeled on either side of the bow in a continuous shimmering vee. Steadily they rowed out alongside the reef until they reached the cardinal marker post with its flashing white light. They had agreed this would be the best spot, as it gave them something to tie up to. Somehow, just doing this seemed an adventure, all

Night fishing

sitting in a dinghy in the middle of the night. Whether or not they caught any fish didn't particularly matter.

Half a kilometre to the south, the salmon farm showed as an outline and a series of yellow flashing buoys. "There's nobody there at night, but security patrols come out occasionally," said Jake.

Fin had just felt his second good bite when they heard an engine. They immediately began to debate whether to show a light, but Zac was sure they were in no risk of being hit by another boat. "Nobody'll come near the reef or this pole," he said. "If they do we can shine the torch at them, ay."

There were two boats, a large one which stayed close in to the shore where it was very dark, and a smaller one with an outboard. It was motoring quietly to the salmon farm. Neither of those boats seemed to have any lights on either. "Probably the security guys," suggested Fin. And then, to Jess's alarm, she heard familiar voices. It is a peculiar fact that when talking over the top of an engine, people speak more loudly. And voices carry a long way over calm water.

"Wonder if those Snake Island kids are still there?" one voice was saying.

"That girl was worth the visit," the other one was saying. "Pity we didn't give her a proper check out!" Then the outboard stopped and they heard people climbing onto one of the fish farm pens and some banging noises.

"It's the black-shirts!" whispered Jess. "What are they up to?"

The others sensed her alarm. "Let's get outta here," said Jake, and not even Fin disagreed. This time they hugged the eastern side of the reef and island, but the trip took long enough for them to hear the smaller boat make a trip to the larger one and then return to the fish farm.

No lights were showing on Tania and Zac's boat, so they

risked quietly hauling the longboat out at Jake's Jetty, seeing that it was high tide and calm. Then, back at camp a pact was made.

"We can't tell any of the adults what happened tonight, ay! Not that it was wrong, but they mightn't realise how safe it was!" Zac had voiced what they all felt, and they agreed with a single murmur.

Chapter 9

Plans are Changed

FOR JAKE AND ZAC, SLEEPING on the bare ground without mattresses, the morning's slow awakening was a painful affair. However, once they had emerged from the bivvy they soon forgot their aches and bruises. The small butterfly birds were flitting about in the trees overhead and Zac was pleased to hear the familiar call of a shining cuckoo.

"We hear that in New Zealand during summer too," he exclaimed.

The girls were late risers too after their midnight adventure. Jess switched her phone on briefly in case of a text message, but there was nothing. She sent off a quick text to reassure her parents they were still completely happy, and checked the battery. It was low. She switched it off until lunchtime.

Over breakfast they began planning their day. Tania and Zac were very quiet, and Jess remembered what their parents had said about sailing down the channel today. "Surely if you talk to them they might let you stay another night?" she said. "After all, are they really in such a hurry to keep moving?"

"I'll call them on the hand-held," said Tania, and they listened to the conversation. "*Moananui, Moananui*, this is shore party, shore party on channel seven seven, do you copy? Over." There was a brief pause.

"Shore party, this is *Moananui*, copy you loud and clear. Over." It was Miriama's distinct Kiwi voice.

"Hi Mum, do we really have to leave today. Is a change of plan possible? Over." There was a longer pause.

"Maybe that could be possible, can you come out to talk about it? Over."

"Okay Mum, we'll be out in half an hour. Over and out." She switched off the radio. "Sounds hopeful," she added, her brown eyes sparkling.

"What does your boat name mean? "Maw-ah-na-noo-ee". Is it a Maori word?" asked Jess.

"Yeah, it means big sea or ocean. The Pacific is 'Te Moananui a Kiwa', meaning Kiwa's ocean. Kiwa was an ancient navigator."

"Can you speak Maori?" asked Fin curiously.

"Not fluently. They teach it at school. Mum knows quite a lot. Her dad is from the east coast." Jess wondered what the significance of the east coast was but Zac broke in to bring them back to matters in hand.

"We won't pull down the sail bivvy till we know if we can stay longer. It'd be awesome if we could go exploring along the shoreline a bit today in your longboat."

Jake looked thoughtful. "Yeah! An expedition to Missionary Bay. There's always good beachcombing at Stockyards beach. But I don't think the longboat's safe enough for five of us going that far. Specially if the sea-breeze gets up this afternoon."

Fin broke in quickly. "P'raps we could take your inflatable too. Then we'll have a tow-boat if we need one." He had been dying for an excuse for a ride in their dinghy.

"That means Mum and Dad'll have no dinghy. Maybe they wouldn't mind. They could pull up the anchor if we needed rescuing, ay. But why not just take *Privateer* as the second boat?" Zac asked.

"Problem is, *Privateer* isn't very good for rowing long distances. And there's no wind yet to sail. The inflatable would be better," explained Jake. He didn't really like admitting that his beautiful new boat was not perfect for every occasion, but he had another idea for their expedition which didn't need *Privateer*. He kept it quiet for the moment.

"Your parents seem like really good sorts," said Jess. "If we can come up with a sensible plan for them, they might stay longer."

"You may be right," agreed Tania. "They've been saying that the only problem about cruising with us kids is that we miss our friends."

"Dad should be back later," added Jess. "I'll need to text him if we do all go exploring. We don't want him freaking out when he realises we're not on the island."

"Maybe you can text him to turn on his VHF and you can talk to him on *Moananui*'s radio," suggested Zac.

"D'you think your parents would mind?" asked Jess. It did seem like a good idea and she would like to talk to her father again.

"Don't see why not," replied Zac. "But we'd better wait and see how they feel about our expedition idea first."

It took nearly an hour before they were climbing aboard *Moananui*. Doing things at a camp always takes time, and they talked their way through breakfast which slowed them down even more. Mike and Miriama didn't seem surprised to see all five of them come alongside in the longboat. Everyone crowded into the big cockpit.

"Have you heard a forecast today Dad?" asked Zac, wondering how best to introduce their proposal.

"Yes. Sounds good for today but it'll be blowing up tomorrow. Sea-breeze forecast again today. Tomorrow afternoon they're expecting strong southerlies." The castaways all looked at each other. Camping in bad weather is not so much fun. And what if Mike and Miriama wanted to sail out today to find a better anchorage? They looked at the adults' faces for a sign of their intentions.

"When's your Dad coming back Jess?" asked Miriama softly. Jess guessed that the twins' parents were possibly unsure about abandoning the three with bad weather coming and no back-up yacht.

"Oh he expects to sail back this afternoon." She looked at Jake, knowing that he didn't want to make their father look stupid by getting a rope around his propeller. On impulse she blurted out the details. "The problem was that he damaged the propeller when he was leaving to come back here, and he had to go up on the slipway to fix it. He wanted to come for us in Doug's runabout but we wouldn't let him. It would've spoilt the camp and we spent so much time planning this holiday."

She could see that they understood exactly what she meant. After all they had children of their own.

"Actually Dad we were wondering – well I suggested it – whether Jess or Jake could use our VHF to talk to their father. She's been texting him a lot but her mobile's nearly flat." Zac was being very diplomatic.

"Of course they can. But will he be listening?"

"He will if I text him and tell him to!" replied Jess immediately. She was aware that nobody had mentioned their day's plans yet, but she would certainly feel better to hear Dad's voice.

While they all watched, she sent off a text to her father.

Hi dad switch on your VHF we will call u

A moment later came the reply.

Will listen on Channel 16 wait 5 mins

"Would anyone like a hot drink while we wait?" asked Miriama. Five hands went up for hot chocolate, and they all climbed down into the main cabin, keen to hear the radio conversation. Mike showed Jess where to sit at the navigation station, and turned the radio to Channel 16, the international calling frequency. "You've used one before have you?" he asked.

"Yes, Dad lets me use ours and I've done the radio course. I want to join the navy," she added. With everyone watching she was slightly nervous. "How do you pronounce your boat name again?" she asked Tania.

"Maw-ah-na-noo-ee," said Tania, running the syllables together. Jess repeated it twice, took a deep breath and pressed the microphone button.

"*Sea Fever, Sea Fever* this is *Moananui, Moananui* on one six," she said and waited. Almost immediately came the reply.

"*Moananui* this is *Sea Fever*, do you copy, over." It was so nice to hear his voice she thought. He had some difficulty pronouncing the Maori name though.

"*Sea Fever* what channel shall we use? Over," Jess asked, remembering that they were not allowed to chat on this one, only make contact.

"Go eight one," came the reply, and she realised he was suggesting the repeater channel high in the hills because most other channels would be affected by the land between the two yachts."

"Going up," she said, and Mike switched the radio up to eighty one for her. She could tell from his expression that he was happy with how she was handling the radio, and she was relieved.

"*Sea Fever* this is *Moananui*," she called after a brief pause, knowing that her father may have trouble remembering the boat name.

"This is *Sea Fever* in reply. How are you Jess? Is anything the matter? Over." Her father was obviously a bit rattled at being called like this. Now that they were on a talk channel she could skip the formalities, she thought.

"Nothing wrong Dad. We're all fine. It's just that we've got the chance to talk from our friends' boat, the Kiwi boat we saw in Kettering. Are you coming this afternoon? Over."

"I certainly hope so. Mum will come too. The new shaft bearing should be ready by lunchtime. But we have to go back in the water by two-thirty or the tide will be too low. Over."

"That's good. We're still fine. Plenty of food left. Don't worry about us. Over."

"Okay Jess, I'll text if there's any change of plan. Give our love to the crew. Over and out."

Jess hesitated. "Bye Dad. This is *Moananui* out."

Everyone started talking, and the kettle began to whistle. Jake was rather disappointed not to have had a chance to talk, but in a way he was relieved. He didn't think he could sound as professional on the radio as Jess or Tania, and there was nothing else that really needed saying anyway. Radios were more a navy thing too. Pirates used other methods.

While the castaways had drinks and biscuits, Mike and Miriama disappeared on deck for a while with Zac. When they came back down Zac was grinning.

"We've decided to stay on for another day," said Mike. "We think it'd be nice to meet your parents this afternoon. And we don't see why Tania and Zac shouldn't be able to camp another night. But we'll need to get away tomorrow morning. I don't want to be caught in this anchorage in a bad southerly."

Fin looked at the others. He hadn't said much today, but now he chipped in. "Can we still go on our expedition?" He had been thinking about the inflatable all morning.

Zac turned to his parents sheepishly. "Actually we have got a plan for today seeing that we're allowed to stay on ..." They all started talking at once. About how it was a perfect day for exploring, how it wasn't really all that far, how they needed the inflatable as well as the longboat, and so on. The twins' parents listened patiently. Finally Miriama spoke for them both.

"It seems as if your parents trust you three to make sensible decisions or you wouldn't be here in the first place. So all we need to do is give permission for Zac and Tania to go with you, and decide whether we can manage without the inflatable for a few hours. What do you think Mike?"

Mike was smiling to himself. "Well if we didn't want our children to go adventuring, we wouldn't have sailed them across the Tasman in the first place. And as for the inflatable, it makes sense for them to take two boats. Their fibreglass dinghy is a bit small for the five of them over that distance, and our one gives them a fast rescue boat too. We can always come down in *Moananui* if they need help. They can call us on the hand-held."

It was settled. They were a happy band of adventurers, rowing back to the island shortly after.

Understandably, Fin wanted to take a fishing rod. "My bait's disappeared," he said, puzzled. "But I can get some oysters for bait and use the spinner."

Zac and Tania didn't have much extra gear to organise at camp, so they helped clean up while the others got organised. They were all in a hurry to get away before the breeze developed. It would be hard work rowing into the wind. Jess gathered up enough food for lunch as well as three water bottles and her windproof jacket. She found the large scale map which showed the whole of Great Bay, and quickly traced the shoreline between Snake Bay and Missionary Bay. She took care to put it into a plastic bag with a pencil.

Jake meanwhile was taking down his blue tarpaulin from where it hung as a cover over the cooking area. When questioned, he was rather vague. "It could be useful as an emergency shelter," he shrugged. As well as his jacket, he added the machete and a bundle of thin ropes. Then they were off.

"Have you got your coat, Fin?" asked Jess before they reached Jake's Jetty.

"Oops," said Fin, and dashed off, hurrying back as they were climbing into the longboat. Rowing out to the steel ketch, they transferred Fin and Tania into the grey inflatable dinghy, complete with fishing rod and the twins' coats and lunches, which Miriama handed down as they cast off.

"Bon voyage. Be back by four or we'll come looking for you. We'll stay listening on channel seventy seven," said Mike. The longboat was already halfway out of the bay, Zac and Jake rowing a zigzag course with an oar each. Fin could hear Jess laughing before Tania started the outboard.

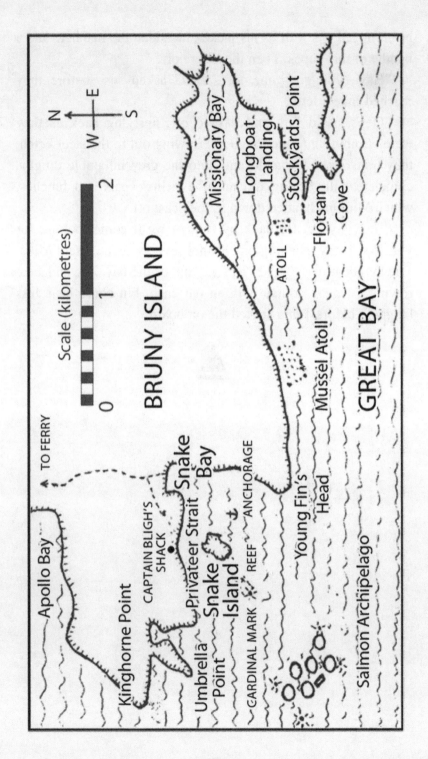

Chapter 10

Expedition

FIN WAS HAVING A GREAT time towing his lure behind the inflatable, but before long Tania slowed down. "We can't waste too much petrol," she explained. "And it'll be more fun staying with the others." She circled around and cut the engine, waiting for the longboat to catch up.

Without any bait, Fin spent the time casting his spinner. "I should've got some oysters off the rocks before we left," he said, but Tania reminded him that it was his fault that he didn't have time because he had to go back for his jacket.

Coming up behind them quite quickly was the longboat. Jess had taken Jake's place and she and Zac were rowing a reasonably straight course. It was still calm.

"It's calm enough for us all to come in the longboat for a while," called Jake. "We can take turns rowing, and tow the inflatable. That way we'll save fuel for a tow home this afternoon. Maybe we can use one of your paddles for a steering oar, then we'll go straighter."

Fin wanted to stay in the inflatable towing his lure so they let him. Tania scrambled into the bigger dinghy with a paddle. It seemed more fun being together, and they made steady progress along the shoreline. It was hot work with the sun blazing out of a clear blue sky.

"I thought Tasmania was supposed to be cold," commented Zac, pausing for a moment to wipe off the sweat. "I might have a swim when we get there."

"Our summers are hot, but you'll cool down when the sea-breeze kicks in," replied Jake.

"We should name some places on our map," suggested Jess after she had moved into the stern to let Tania do some rowing. She pulled out her tracing of the shore. With it came the crumpled scrap of photocopied map that she had picked up on the afternoon they were searching for a campsite.

"Here's a treasure map for you Jake," she laughed. "It's even got a couple of crosses on it!"

Jake seized it eagerly, examining how it had clearly torn along a fold. Once he realised that it was part of a recent photocopy he tried to hide his disappointment.

"Not very old," he said, trying to sound interested. "You didn't make it up yourself to trick me did you?"

"No way!" retorted Jess indignantly. "I found it up near that grotty old hut when we arrived. I did tell you about it but you were more interested in finding a cannibal campsite."

"What say we call that headland back there 'Young Fin's Head'," suggested Zac, anxious to avoid an argument. They looked at him, puzzled, so Tania explained, resting on her oar while Jake took over Zac's oar.

"Back on the east coast there's a point called 'Young Nick's Head'," she said. "Captain Cook named it after Nick Young, his cabin boy." Jess smiled and set to work writing it onto her map.

"I s'pose we can't really change names of places already here," said Zac.

"Not too many unless it's something special that has happened to us," said Jess. "But we could change things a bit, like 'Midnight marker' for the reef cardinal mark."

"No way! We don't want any grown-ups seeing that and asking questions about why we called it that, do we?" reacted Jake quickly. Just then there was a shout from Fin.

"I've got something! It's big." His rod was bending and the reel tension was slipping as he wound busily on the handle.

"You'd better not land anything in the inflatable," called Zac. "It'll be too hard to clean out the blood!" The others had stopped rowing and Zac was pulling in the painter to bring Fin alongside the bigger dinghy. Fin passed the rod to Zac and climbed in to finish reeling it in.

"It's a kahawai," yelled Zac.

"No, it's an Australian salmon," corrected Fin as he reeled it alongside. "Wish I had a gaff. My line's gonna break if I lift it."

"Here, pass the bucket and I'll scoop it aboard like a landing net," suggested Zac. After two attempts he had it flapping in the bottom of the dinghy, along with half a bucket of bloody water.

"Bang it on the head ..."

"Bleed it straight away ..."

"Stop it splashing – I'm getting covered with blood ..."

"Get it away from my toes ..." They were all babbling at once. Fin seemed to be the most level-headed about it all. In a moment he had it upside down and bleeding quietly in the bucket.

Australian kahawai

"See – it's an Australian salmon," he announced. "Look at its spots and the shape of its mouth. About two kilo I reckon."

"Well in New Zealand we call that fish a kahawai," retorted Zac. "Trust you Aussies to claim a kahawai as Australian! It should taste the same anyway. Pity we can't light a fire ashore and cook it up for lunch."

Tania hated having slimy red water under her feet, so they mopped it out as best they could. Fin insisted on being towed behind again in case there were more to catch. Before they started rowing they looked around them.

"Look – there's a sea eagle!" exclaimed Jess excitedly. Following her gaze they could clearly see a huge white-bellied bird lazily circling not far from Young Fin's Head. Even from that distance its dark wings were far larger than the biggest seagull.

"Cool! I haven't ever seen an eagle" murmured Zac in awe. "Only hawks."

"We did have a giant eagle in New Zealand hundreds of years ago but it's extinct now," added Tania.

"We've got wedgetails as well and they're even bigger," crowed Fin from the inflatable behind them.

Tiny ripples were appearing on the water ahead, as a sign of a developing sea-breeze. Just inside the bay ahead were a number of black floats in long rows, with big yellow buoys around them.

Sea eagle

"Mussel rafts," exclaimed Zac. "We've got dozens of those back home in the Marlborough Sounds."

"What are Sounds?" asked Jess.

"They're long inlets like your channel here but bigger," he replied.

"And windier," added Tania.

"There's often good fishing near mussel farms," added Zac, speaking much more quietly, "but don't tell Fin or we'll have no peace." Jess began marking the mussel farm on her map.

"We'll have to think of a better name for it. What about mussel atoll? Makes it seem like we're real explorers finding coral islands in the Pacific."

"Yeah. We could call the salmon farm an archipelago. The fish pens look like a whole lot of round atolls, ay," agreed Zac enthusiastically.

Jake and Tania started rowing again. There were only a few hundred metres to go across Missionary Bay, and they were keen to get there before the head wind developed. Ashore, the bush had been replaced by farmland with a few scattered trees. Some sheep could be seen, but the grass looked brown and dry.

"Your sheep here look grey compared with our white Kiwi ones," commented Zac. "Maybe it's all the dust."

As they rowed into the shallow water near the beach, Tania suddenly let go of her oar and shrieked. "Did you see that – a stingray! I scared it with my oar and it took off." It had left a cloud of muddy water behind in the spot where it had been lurking on the bottom.

"Sit down Fin," yelled Jake, seeing Fin jumping up excitedly in the smaller boat astern. They could make out a dark patch in the water moving rapidly away.

"Smaller than my one," crowed Fin. "Mine was a real monster."

"I'm not wading off this beach," said Tania. It had given her such a fright she was shivering. By now, even though they had stopped rowing, the two boats had glided close to the stony beach. Zac pulled the inflatable alongside and climbed in carrying the short aluminium oar they had been steering the bigger boat with. After checking that the outboard was tilted right up, the others cast off the tow rope so that he and Fin could paddle themselves the last few metres to a place which was clear of oysters. The tide was quite high by now, which was a help as they didn't need to carry the inflatable very far up the beach.

They were going to drag the longboat up too but Zac stopped them. "Why don't we moor it out a bit so we don't have to drag it back down when the tide's dropped. We can use the dinghy anchor and some of your rope, Jake." He showed them how to make a mooring using an old orange-drink bottle off the beach for a float, tied to the anchor which they dropped fifteen metres out from the water's edge. They rigged a long thin piece of Jake's rope for an endless looped line through the handle of the float, and tied the bow of the dinghy to the knot in the line. Then, after rowing back to the shore and climbing out, they pulled on the endless line and watched the longboat glide out to the buoy.

"I wish we'd known about that trick when we arrived at Snake Island," said Jess.

"Think of all the effort it would've saved, instead of dragging it up and down the rocks. We'll do it tonight," said Jake as he tied

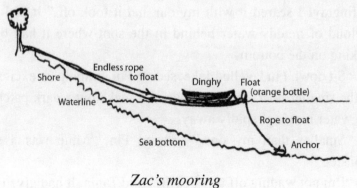

Zac's mooring

86

off the end of the long double rope to a log on the stony beach. "Now let's go beachcombing. There's always good stuff here."

"I'm hungry," said Fin, and Jess rolled her eyes.

"You're always hungry," she growled. "And you weren't even rowing!" But he had drawn their attention to their stomachs and that it was already late morning, so they decided to have a snack – which ended up being most of their lunch. While they ate, Jake was looking along the beach. He could see something orange-coloured near the low point which separated them from the sandy little bay to their south.

"If we split up into two groups we could search a bigger area," he suggested, but could see immediately from their faces that everyone would far rather stay together. Thinking about it, he decided it was more fun in a group. Once they had started walking along the shoreline they spread out a little so that they could examine different parts of the stony beach and the bank above the high tide mark. But they kept within easy talking distance and often came together to look at small things that had been discovered.

Tania particularly liked the shells. There were quite a few that she didn't recognise from New Zealand. One large shell looked familiar though. "Look, here's a sort of paua shell, Zac," she called. He came to see.

"It's a bit different," he commented. "Pinker, and not as nice inside." Jake glanced into Tania's hand.

"It's an ab," he said. "Abalone shell. Good eating. Divers make a fortune here collecting those. They're mostly exported though."

"In New Zealand the paua meat's sold and the shells are used for jewelry," said Tania. "Grandad loves free-diving for them. There's plenty on the east coast. He gets them off the rocks with a screwdriver and brings them home to barbecue. They look gross coz the meat's quite black but they taste nice."

"Usually he beats them up with a hammer and cooks them whole, but I like them sliced up, fried in butter," added Zac.

They spread out again. Jake found the orange object which turned out to be a tangle of frayed ropes, probably from a fishing boat. Fin found a piece of net which he insisted on keeping. Jess found some short wide flat planks which she put in a clear patch so that she could pick them up on the way back later. They would make a good extension for the camp table.

"We should put all our things here for now," she suggested. "Saves us carrying them there and back." So Fin added his net, Tania her shell collection and Jake threw in some pieces of rope he had picked up. They laid a pole out so that it pointed to the pile in case they had difficulty finding it later.

Zac was wandering around among the tussock on the bank above the high tide mark. Suddenly he let out a yelp and they saw him jump backwards in alarm. "Snake!" he yelled. "What do I do?"

"Did it bite you?" yelled Jess back, horrified.

"No, but it's wriggled under that clump there. It's the first one I've ever seen. It's as thick as my arm! Will there be any more here?" He was close to panic.

"You'll be okay. Just keep away from it. Probably the only one." Jess seemed quite relaxed about it. Zac quickly jumped down the bank to where the others stood.

"And I've got bare legs. Do you think it was poisonous?"

"All Tasmanian snakes are poisonous," said Jess, much to his horror. "What colour was it, brown or black?"

"Shiny black and all scaly," he said. "Ugh." He shuddered at the memory.

"Tiger snake," said Jake immediately. "It's related to the cobra. The other big type here's the copperhead but they're browner."

"What'd we have done if he was bitten?" asked Tania, clearly shaken.

"Shiny black and all scaly!"

"We get taught at school," said Jess. "Hardly anyone dies these days. You have to bind it firmly all up and down your leg or arm or wherever was bitten, to stop the poison spreading. It spreads just under the skin you see. Then we'd use your radio or my phone to get help. Maybe they'd send a chopper. You'd probably survive anyway, bound up like that, specially if you kept still. At hospital they can inject anti-venine to neutralise the poison but usually they just wait and see."

"What happens if it bites you on the bum?" asked Fin mischievously. "It'd be hard to bind that up, 'specially if you're fat."

"It's not funny actually. Someone died when that happened once, but she was too embarrassed to ask for help." They were quiet for a moment. "How many people die each year from snake bites?" asked Tania.

"Only about one every ten years in Tasmania nowadays," said Jess. "Like we said yesterday, jack jumper ants are the biggest killers here."

For the next quarter hour they noticed that their Kiwi friends stayed close by them, and watched every step they took. Jake was walking near the bank now, clearly looking for something particular. At last he found it. "Look, come here," he said and they crowded over. A string of quite large ants was scurrying in and out of a hole. He poked the hole with a stick and immediately most of the ants turned and began to attack the stick. They were zigzagging around and hopping off the ground.

"Jack jumpers. Vicious little things. They sting rather than bite. If you see any, keep clear of them."

"Can they really kill people?" asked Tania, amazed that something so small could be so dangerous.

"Only if you're allergic to them," replied Jess. "That's about one person out of ten. And usually they will have been bitten several times before they became allergic. Mum and Dad gave us an epi-pen in case one of us gets bitten and has a fit. Apparently it happens really quickly. Your tongue swells up and stops you breathing."

"What's an epi-pen," asked Tania.

"It's like a pen. You jab the sharp bit into your leg up here and it gives you a drug to stop the fi…"

"Adrenaline, that's what the drug is," interrupted Jake. He knew all about this stuff too and didn't want to be left out. One or two jack jumpers were running up the stick towards his hand, so he dropped the stick and stepped back hastily. The others did the same.

"Let's kill the nasty things," said Fin eagerly.

"Why?" retorted Jess. "They're not hurting anyone here, just defending their nest like they're supposed to. We should just leave them alone and keep moving." She looked at her watch. "It's after one o'clock. I'll give Dad a text and tell him where we are so they don't have a fit if they beat us back to the island and find we've gone." She switched on her phone and tapped out a quick message.

Hi dad and mum we r at missionary exploring. Don't worry we r
safe. have backup boat. C u at snake is later love from the crew.

She left it on for a reply as they moved off further along the
shore and over the low neck of land into the sandier little bay to
the south. Dad's reply when it came seemed rather panicky.

Hi jess not good here. Still waiting for bearing. Will miss tide
if it doesn't come soon. Bugger bugger. You be careful. Will
text again. Love

She read it to the others. "He's not happy," she said. "He
wouldn't normally say 'bugger' like that. I suppose he's heard
about the gale tomorrow afternoon." They walked on, more
quietly. "We'll be fine though. It's just that I know they'll worry."

Their last piece of flotsam on the beach had them all curious.
It looked like some sort of light inside a clear plastic cylinder
about a hundred millimetres in diameter. It had floated ashore so
must have been sealed up when it was made. A black square on
the domed top surface looked like a tiny solar panel. Zac wanted
to break it open to get out the solar panel but Jess insisted that
they keep it whole. She thought their father might like to see it
before they pulled it apart.

"We could call this small beach 'Flotsam Cove', maybe,"
suggested Jess and there was a general murmur of approval.

As they walked back to the boats, they could feel the sea-
breeze on their right cheeks. "Tail-wind home," observed Jake
looking pleased and curiously excited. He had picked up two
long thin poles off the beach and was carrying them on his
shoulder. He couldn't wait to impress them all with the plan he
had kept secret all morning.

Chapter 11

The Rescue Boat is Rescued

WHILE THEY ATE THE REST of their lunch, Jake set to work with the poles, lashing them together like a cross. They watched him curiously. "Who are you going to bury?" asked Zac. "Looks like a grave-marker." Saying nothing, Jake unfolded the blue tarpaulin and began lashing it to the cross pole. Suddenly Jess realised what he was up to.

"It's a sail isn't it? You're rigging a squaresail. What a cool idea." They all joined him to help. The blue tarp was too long for the mast pole, so they rolled it up at the bottom. Jake tied three ropes to the top of the makeshift mast to be used as stays. They tied two more to the end of the cross-pole (the 'yard' Jake insisted it was to be called), and some short ropes to the bottom corners to control the sail.

The tide had begun to drop when they pulled the longboat ashore on the endless line. There was an argument about where to tie the mast side-stay ropes. Jake wanted to thread them through the rowlock holes but Jess refused to let him.

"We have to be able to start rowing quickly if there's an emergency," she argued. "If we can't tie them to something else then I'm not going to sail." She was absolutely determined about that, and finally Jake reluctantly let her tie them to the sides of the rowing seat.

"It won't work as well that way," he sulked. "And they might slip in to the middle."

"Too bad," she retorted. "Use a rolling hitch. If it doesn't work then we row. Or get a tow from Zac and Tania like we planned." After several attempts the mast seemed to stand up safely, with the sail flapping quite hard in the freshening sea-breeze. They all wanted to sail in the longboat but in the end Zac agreed to drive the inflatable. He planned to stay close enough to them so that they could still talk.

"Take my mobile in this plastic bag," offered Jess. "It'll probably be safer with you anyway in case we capsize. Then you can take a photo of us with it. Make sure you switch it off afterwards to save the battery."

They pulled themselves out to the mooring where Jess untied it and hauled up the anchor. The wind was blowing them away from the shore. As soon as Tania and Fin pulled in the sheets the sail stopped flogging and filled. Jake sat in the stern with a steering oar. He was in heaven.

"I got a good picture," they heard Zac call as he pushed off the inflatable and lowered the outboard. The next moment they heard him yell. He sounded really upset.

"Let go the sheets," said Jess and the sail began to flog again. She leapt into the rowing seat with the oars and began slowly rowing backwards towards Zac who was drifting towards them.

"I hit a rock with the propeller," explained Zac. He looked terrible. "The engine works fine but the prop won't spin at all." It was a disaster. He wondered whether they should call *Moananui* to come and rescue them.

"Throw us your painter and we'll see what it's like towing you," suggested Jake. Before long they had Zac under tow. He had raised the outboard out of the water to reduce the drag, but

Jake was finding it much harder to steer because the tow line drag was preventing him from turning. "It'll be easier to steer if you come in our boat," he called, so Zac was pulled alongside and climbed in. They knew that this was not what had been planned, with all five aboard in a freshening sea-breeze, but having an extra person aboard seemed to make the longboat more steady, and the inflatable had hardly any drag now, being towed empty. In fact it was blowing along behind them at almost the same speed. Jake found it easy to steer again.

"It's hard holding the steering oar down in the water," he complained after a while. "We'll have to take turns. Also I think we could experiment using the towline to help with steering." Sure enough they found that shifting the tow rope from one side to the other helped change the direction they were going, and before long they only needed to use the steering oar for small adjustments.

The longboat sailed steadily under her 'jury rig' as Jake called it. His only regret was that he hadn't brought the pirate flag to fly. They took great care to sit where the boat balanced best. Fin was in the bow, being lightest, and the three who weren't steering took turns to sit on the middle seat or crouch in the bottom. It was rather wet there, as a few splashes were coming in over the stern. They made a rule that whoever was in the bottom would bail out the puddle there.

"We're easily going as fast as we were when we rowed here," observed Jake after they were well past the mussel atoll. Young Fin's Head could be seen up ahead now. Just then, Jess's mobile beeped. Another text, she thought, feeling an empty space in her pocket. Zac sheepishly handed it to her in the plastic bag he had put in his coat pocket, apologising for forgetting to turn it off.

Bolting the bearing in now but will be too late for tide. Will your batteries stand a talk?

Jess looked at the battery indicator. Very low but she could try. Crouching in the bottom of the dinghy, away from any spray, she phoned her father.

"Hi love," he said immediately. "Look we've done our best but we're not going to get off now till the tide is coming in late tomorrow morning. We'll definitely be ready then. How are you guys? Should we come tonight for you with Doug?"

"No Dad, it'll be perfect if you just leave it till tomorrow." She wondered if he had heard the forecast but she simply couldn't bear finishing this adventure so tamely in a fizz-boat. "We've got tons of food and water left on the island. When you get here tomorrow we can have the camp packed up ready so we can go sailing down the channel for a few days. Honestly we're having such a great time."

A larger than normal wave slopped over the stern and she wondered what he would say if he could see them now. The others looked at her, their eyes showing how much they agreed with her. Jake was thinking what fun it would be to do some sailing together with the Kiwi ketch later in the week. From their faces, Zac and Tania seemed to share his feelings.

Her phone battery alarm was beeping. "Mobile's going dead Dad. See you and Mum tomorrow. Love you," she blurted out quickly but it had gone silent. Their link was gone. From now on it was only the VHF radio, but Dad may not be listening to that. No worries, she thought to herself. They'll be here in twenty-four hours and we'll be fine.

She would not have felt quite so confident if she had known what those next hours had in store.

Mike and Miriama watched them sailing around Young Fin's Head and into the anchorage. The castaway sailors had to brace the yard around and sit on one side, as the wind was more on their starboard side now. As they came near to *Moananui* they could see Mike taking pictures with a big lens on his camera.

"You look magnificent ..."

"You look magnificent," he called into the wind. "That modern thing you're towing spoils the effect a bit though."

As they lowered the mast and rowed the last short distance to the steel ketch, Jess noticed a sea kayak hauled up on the southern stony beach of the island. She was too busy fitting the oars to pay much attention.

Zac admitted the outboard disaster as soon as he was aboard. He had been worrying about it all the way home. If he had broken the gearbox it would make a lot of trouble for them during their Australian cruise. They needed the outboard to get ashore. The inflatable was very hard to row when it was windy. He wished that they had brought a solid dinghy like the longboat which was so much better to row.

His father listened carefully when he told what had happened and asked a couple of specific questions. Finally he spoke. "Sounds like you just broke a sheer-pin," he said, looking as relaxed as ever. "I should have explained how to fix that." They lifted the outboard up on deck and he brought them all around to show them. "There's a weak little pin that holds the prop to the shaft," he continued. "It's designed to break if you hit a rock or anything, and saves the gears from being damaged. There are spare ones here," and he showed them two small rods like short nails under the engine cover. "To fix the problem you just take the prop off like this," and he undid the split-pin behind the propeller. "The new one slides in here and presto, you're in business again." Jess glanced at Zac and could see the relief written all over his face.

"We haven't seen your parents' boat yet," Miriama began. "Did you say it's blue?"

"Oh, yes, I talked to Dad on the mobile just before. They got the bearing bolted on but it arrived too late to get off the slipway till tomorrow's rising tide before lunch. They'll come straight here then. Dad wanted to pick us up in Doug's boat but we wouldn't let him. It'd ruin our last night of camping."

"It's going to blow tomorrow afternoon," said Mike.

"Yes but we'll have everything packed up by the time they arrive, to save time," said Jess quickly. "Then we're going cruising further down the channel for a few days. We might even be able to join you there." She was trying to hide her eagerness but realised she probably hadn't.

"Someone's been on the island with a sea kayak," said Miriama, changing the subject. "We watched him through the binoculars. He seems to be wandering around with some sort of map." Jake's ears pricked up immediately.

"Did he have red hair?" he asked eagerly, thinking back to his mystery treasure hunter.

Mike screwed up his face, trying to remember. "Not sure, but he did have a beard. It's hard to tell from this far away."

Jess reacted in a more practical way. She was thinking more about their camp. They had gone and left everything there for anyone just to walk in and snoop around. She tried to remember what things would be worthwhile for someone to pinch.

"We can still camp ashore tonight can't we?" asked Tania, and was relieved when her parents confirmed what they had agreed to earlier.

"We'll keep the inflatable out here so we can get to you if you need us," said Mike.

"I've packed you some more food for tonight and breakfast," said Miriama. "Is there anything you other castaways need that you're short of?"

"Not really," said Jess quickly, thinking hard. "We packed enough stores for a week. There'll be enough water for another night. Maybe a loaf of bread would help though. Ours is going mouldy and we were relying on getting a bit more from *Sea Fever*."

Miriama handed them the supplies as they all climbed into the longboat. They decided to land on the gravel beach at the north end to avoid the surge at Jake's jetty. "We'll moor it off with the endless rope," said Jake. "Much better that way."

The sea kayak was pulled up near where they rigged up the mooring. It was a red fibreglass one. There was no sign of its owner. However as they carried their things back to camp they saw him, studying a map and looking at the ground and up a tree. He had a short red beard and quite long hair. As soon as he saw them he looked startled and put his map under his jacket, hurrying away nervously. Jake was sure it was the same man he had seen here a year ago.

"He's certainly acting strangely," observed Tania. "I wonder what he's up to?" They waited to watch him, and shortly after noticed him lifting his kayak into the water and paddling off towards the deaf old angry man's shack.

"Maybe he's linked up with Captain Bligh," suggested Jake. "Perhaps they've both been searching for the coins. That could be why he wants to ban campers." They watched him carry his sea kayak up the beach to the shack, before they turned and walked back to camp. On the way, Jake told the others about the lost treasure of the shipwrecked *Hope*, and his theory on where it may be.

As usual, Fin had rushed ahead, and they had barely reached the clearing when he ran back to meet them. "Someone's been snooping in my tent," he declared angrily.

Chapter 12

Suspicions Grow

FIN'S DOME TENT HAD DEFINITELY been disturbed. The food pile was spread out and even his clothes looked like they had been messed up. "It looks as if someone's been getting into the pockets of that smelly old fishing sweatshirt," he complained bitterly. "I hope it made him stink too."

Jess was quite upset. It spoiled the pleasure of the camp to think of someone poking around. It was as if they had been violated, the same feeling she had after the black-shirt men had hassled her. She unzipped her tent and looked around. Nothing seemed particularly different from how she had left it, but she couldn't be sure. Perhaps her clothes were in a different place. Tania couldn't remember how her things had been left either. They had gone in such a hurry this morning.

"Are you sure you zipped up your tent when you left?" she asked Fin curiously.

"Definitely," replied Fin remembering doing it the first time when they had all left. He had been in a rush when he came back just afterwards for his coat, and he wasn't so sure about then. But Jess would be mad with him if he had left his tent unzipped with all the food in it. He thought he probably must have zipped it up then too.

Zac and Jake had a look in their bivvy too. It was so hard to tell if anything had changed. They had left it in a mess anyway. Jake checked that his shovel and machete were still there. They were.

"What do you think he was looking for?" asked Tania.

"Maybe he thought we had a map or had dug up the treasure," suggested Jake. "He might have seen the holes I dug even though I filled them in and covered them with leaves. Anyway he's gone off empty-handed now and good riddance. We'll call him 'Redbeard' though I don't know if he deserves the honour of being given a pirate name."

High above their heads in the trees, some large birds were screeching, a harsh shrill sound that was being relayed from tree to tree. Looking up they could clearly see a flock of huge black parrots with long fan-shaped yellow tails. They were clumsily flapping from branch to branch, attacking the bark with their beaks. Pieces of bark and even small branches were being crunched up or snapped off and falling to the ground. "Cockies," said Jake. "Black cockatoos. They come down from the hills when the weather's going to pack up. They eat grubs in the branches."

"Our mountain parrots are called keas," said Zac. "They love chewing up cars – particularly all the plastic and rubber bits on the outside!" They all laughed, and only Jess thought about the bad weather these birds may be forewarning.

There was still some of the afternoon left, and they began talking about what to do next. "Tania and I haven't even explored this island properly yet," Zac reminded them, so they set off around the island showing all the places of interest. Fin was eager to show them Stingray Rock, and then they had to see where Jake had been digging for treasure. Jake told them his methods of searching out the soft patches. They had seen Jake's Jetty already of course. When they investigated the old hut Tania screwed up her nose. "I'd never try sleeping in here," she said, pointing to the open holes in the walls and the large section of open floor.

They had to step around broken bottles as they picked their way towards the open grass to the north. Zac noticed a small muddy pond and commented. "There's probably water here in winter, ay. It's nearly dry now though." They had seen the black-shirts' fireplace yesterday, so they stopped at the old pond while Jess explained how she was measuring the island.

"I'm only doing to the highwater mark, and haven't finished yet," she said, so Tania offered to help with the tape and pegs. Fin went off to try fishing on the west side for an hour while the others busied themselves.

Zac and Jake both studied Jess's piece of ripped map. It could easily have been part of the island as there was clearly a shoreline along one edge, but there were no other clues. Probably somewhere along the western side. The two hand-drawn crosses could just be someone's guesses. There was nothing to indicate what they represented.

Zac was keen to try digging around in the campsite clearing. "It's a logical place really coz it's the highest part of the island," he reasoned. Jake wasn't quite so sure that it was a good idea. He had already tried a few places around the camp and found the dirt as hard as rock. "What say we dig out a few big rocks and check under them," suggested Zac. That was a new tactic that Jake hadn't thought of, so they set about locating where there were big flat stones just below the surface. It was worth considering, because hiding treasure under flat rocks would be one way for pirates and robbers to put off treasure hunters.

Jake was worried about snapping his shovel handle levering up big rocks. After all, it was only a light camping shovel. So they worked out a method of digging the hard dirt away from the edge of the rock with the shovel, and then using the two poles they had used for the longboat jury rig to lever the rocks up. It was hard work, and twice they snapped the end off the longest pole. Underneath each rock was more hard ground and after five rocks had been investigated they began to get tired.

The sixth rock immediately seemed different. It was flat but when they levered it up it came away as a rectangular small slab leaving a straight edge next to it. They brushed it off and immediately it became obvious what it was.

"It's a brick!" exclaimed Zac. "An old one though. Look at the surface. You can see shells in it. Probably homemade." They eagerly dug up the one next to it, and the next. They could see an old rusty pipe in the dirt beneath.

"Maybe this was part of that family's house, the one that was attacked by convicts," suggested Jake, rather disappointedly. "There won't be any treasure here. That place would've been built later than the wreck." They poked around with the shovel and a stick for a while and worked out the rough area covered by the bricks. It was rectangular, and they guessed it was probably where the original chimney and hearth had been. Jake thought the chimney bricks would have been taken away years ago. Anyway they were rather sick of treasure hunting by now, so after putting the bricks back they went off to find the girls.

They found Tania and Jess nearly at the end of a very long north-south transect line measurement. They were quite tired too. It had been a long day. "It's much quicker with two people," commented Jess. "And more fun with someone to talk to. You should hear what Tania said about the wind in Wellington. People often have to hold onto lampposts and her sunglasses blew off her face once."

"Yeah and we never found them again," added Zac. "Dad says a man was in a phone box once when the whole box blew over." They laughed, though it wasn't funny for the poor man, thought Jess.

"Was he badly hurt?" she asked.

"Not too badly I think," replied Zac. "House roofs often blow off too, and even high-rise windows have blown out. That's pretty dangerous."

"What about earthquakes?" asked Jake. "I've heard about what happened to one of your cities over there too."

"Oh we get them all the time," said Tania casually. "Most of the big new buildings are built on ball-bearings to stop them shaking too badly."

"You're joking aren't you?" asked Jess, dumbfounded.

"She's sort of right," replied Zac, "though they aren't exactly ball bearings – mainly rubber and lead. You can go under the museum building and see them. They say Wellington's overdue for a big quake that'll destroy the main motorway, and Christchurch was knocked around really badly."

"And you guys are scared of our little snakes," laughed Jake. "I'd rather live here in Tassie any day than your scary country!"

The laughter was good for them. They all walked back to camp much happier than they were an hour earlier. Nobody mentioned Redbeard for the rest of the evening. Fin came back without any fish. He was disappointed, but at least he had filletted the Australian kahawai (as they agreed to call it) to fry as part of their dinner. When Tania opened Miriama's food package they were surprised to see an enormous bacon and egg pie, enough for them all.

"Good old Mum," said Zac and they all agreed. Jess cooked up a big rice pudding with lots of milk powder and dried fruit for dessert. The light was fading and it was completely calm as they sat on the camp log seats eating their dessert. In the west the water had turned to silver and the trees and bushes looked dark against the background. The sky was beginning to turn slightly golden.

"I wonder if we'll have a red sunset – you know, 'red sky at night, sailor's delight'," said Tania.

"It's supposed to be stormy tomorrow afternoon," Zac reminded her. And surely enough as they talked and watched, the sky slowly faded from gold to darkness.

Last evening at the campsite

JESS DIDN'T SLEEP well that night. She had a feeling that somehow she may have done something wrong. For hours as she dozed and tossed and turned she thought about tomorrow afternoon's gale warning and how she had turned down her father's offer of a safe ride home yesterday. What if things did go wrong? She knew it was really her selfishness in wanting to stay on, camping with their new friends, that had driven her to persuade her father not to come in Doug's boat. What if somebody got hurt? What if the gale came early? What if they were stuck on the island with no food left because she had refused to accept a ride home for them?

Somewhere not far from the tents after midnight she could make out some faint scratching noises, and twice she heard twigs breaking. She wondered if there were any possums on the island. The biggest problem for any large creature would be a shortage of water in summer. She had heard that that was why this sort of island was often free of rats. Once on a mainland camp they had a problem with rats and possums getting into their food. In this camp the main reason she liked the food tent to be zipped up was to keep flies and creepy crawlies out.

It was hot in the tent, so she unzipped the door and looked around. There on the table where they had left it at dinner time was the solar light they had found on the beach. It was flashing orange in a regular rhythm – on, off two, three, on, off, two, three ... Just as well Zac didn't smash it, she thought. She would tell them about it in the morning.

She tried to work out in her head when *Sea Fever* would arrive at the anchorage. She knew that their boat could only get on or off the slipway during the period of time about two hours either side of high tide. Yesterday's limit on the falling tide was two-thirty so that meant the earliest the boat would float off the cradle would be shortly after eleven. That meant if they motored straight over they could show up here at about twelve. Surely that would be all right. After all, the wind wasn't supposed to get strong until the afternoon. She slept a little better after that.

It was as calm as a millpond next morning when they woke. Tania was first up, eager to boil some water on Jess's camp stove. She wanted to make the most of the last few hours on the island. She could hear the older two boys groaning under their sail about bruises and sore bones and she felt even more pleased that she had been able to use Jake's mattress. This camp was awesome fun.

Fin was up soon after and for once he didn't rush off with his fishing rod. He sat near the cooker and asked Tania about New Zealand. He didn't know much about it, mainly that there were two islands and a few cities and that it was quite a lot like Tasmania. He was particularly interested in the places her family usually sailed, and when she told him about Cook Strait with its strong winds and fast currents he became quite excited. "One day we might sail there," he said. "What's the fishing like?"

Tania was not particularly keen on fishing but she could remember quite a few times they had tried drift-fishing in places like Tory Channel and Cape Jackson. "We've caught plenty of gummy sharks and some hideous fish like grunters and Maori chiefs," she said. "They have nasty sharp spikes that can make your fingers go septic. Most of the time we just catch spotties and cod and sometimes snapper. You can get them over the side of the boat on anchor."

Fin started telling her about his best catches, slightly enlarged to make them sound even better. But before he had got very far the other boys emerged, yawning from the bivvy.

"Nice morning, ay," said Zac, stretching as he peered up at the blue sky through the unmoving trees. "No wind yet, that's good." They peered out through the trees for a filtered view of the water. "It's like a mirror. Maybe there's not going to be a gale at all today." Hearing them talk, Jess stirred and crawled out of her tent. She was feeling rather grumpy after her bad night's sleep, but the sight of Zac's cheerful face and wild curly hair made her feel a bit better.

"Perhaps we can finish the map this morning," she suggested to Tania. "We could pack up the campsite first after breakfast, and pile everything up at Jake's Jetty all ready to take out to the boats at lunchtime."

"Yeah and we could have one last crack at the treasure," suggested Jake.

"And I can try out that rock between the jetty and Stingray Rock. It's the only good place I haven't tried yet. I might catch some lunch to take back to *Sea Fever*," added Fin.

As soon as breakfast was over, Zac rowed the longboat out to *Moananui* to arrange for them to stay on the island until *Sea Fever* arrived at lunchtime. Mike was slightly hesitant about leaving it too late, but Miriama agreed with Zac.

"Let them have their fun, dear," she said. "It's so calm this morning that it's hardly likely to start blowing much before lunch. Then we can meet the castaways' parents before we sail after lunch." Mike was not sufficiently concerned to argue the point, and decided to spend the morning cleaning the engine and doing some routine maintenance.

Meanwhile Jake had rigged *Privateer* ready to sail out to the reef at lunchtime to meet his parents as they sailed in. After Zac had returned and pulled the longboat back out to its new mooring, Jake got him to help lift *Privateer* down to a good place just below the high-water mark. They decided to leave the sail up, idly swinging in the lightest puffs of wind. Glancing across the channel they noticed grey clouds above the hills slowly moving towards them. "I hope the sun stays out this morning," said Jake.

As the boys began walking back to camp, the noise of an outboard motor caught their attention. It was coming from the Snake Bay shore and, turning to look, they noticed a flat-bottomed aluminium punt leaving the beach near Captain Bligh's shack. Feeling too exposed, Jake and Zac hurried into the shelter of the thick undergrowth to watch. Very soon they could see who the two occupants were. One had red hair, and the other grey.

"Redbeard and Captain Bligh," declared Jake, nervously. "What do they want?" The punt was clearly going to come ashore somewhere near *Privateer*, and soon from their hiding place they watched Redbeard climb out into the shallow water lifting a pack and what looked like a large metal cage. What really startled them was the third item, which Captain Bligh was handing over. It was clearly a rifle. Then as they watched, the grey haired older man started the outboard and with only a brief wave, motored steadily away in the direction of his shack.

Back at camp, they held an emergency meeting. "What's he up to?" asked Jess, echoing what everyone was thinking. They all talked at once, but looking at his watch, Jake stopped them.

"Let's finish breaking camp now," he said. "We have to take everything to the jetty no matter what happens. Maybe your parents have seen Redbeard already. But anyway once we've done that then maybe we'll have a better idea what he's up to."

"Nobody can take any risks from now on," added Jess. "We have to stick together. He might be a dangerous criminal."

Chapter 13

Danger Everywhere

ABOARD *MOANANUI*, MIKE WAS TOO busy down in the engine compartment to notice the line of angry grey clouds rolling towards them. Miriama was in the main cabin trying to finish her book in peace and quiet before her kids returned with all their usual noisy demands. On the island, Zac and Tania were busy with their castaway friends, packing up the camp and piling the gear near Jake's Jetty. They had posted Fin as the lookout to make sure Redbeard wasn't sneaking up on them. With all their focus on the eastern side, the threatening grey wall rapidly approaching from the west was hidden behind the canopy of trees. It was not until a loud rumble of thunder startled them that they noticed how dark the entire western sky had become. And it was only half past ten. Almost immediately came the first puff of wind, quickly followed by a stronger one and a few spatters of rain. They could hear the trees on the south-west side of the island start to roar.

"*Privateer*!! Quick," yelled Jake and raced off towards where he had left his precious boat fully rigged on the stony northern beach. The others dropped whatever they were carrying and tore after him. If they kept together they should be safe. Who could be sure that Redbeard wasn't planning to take a hostage?

Zac remembered the hand-held radio in his coat pocket. It would be in the sailbag with his spare clothes. He tried to remember whether he had switched it off yesterday when they returned from their expedition. As he ran with the others behind Jake he wondered how long the radio batteries would last if it had been left on without transmitting.

Through the trees near the track they could see Redbeard, looking startled at the sight of all five of them racing along the trail. He seemed to be trying to avoid being near the castaways. Jake, pounding along the trail, was more concerned with trying to see if *Privateer* had blown on her side. As they cleared the thicker area of scrub and ran down the gentle grassy slope towards the shore he saw to his relief that the Optimist was still standing, though the new red sail was flapping wildly and making a deafening crackling sound. It was lucky he had left the mainsheet loose, he thought, and that this part of the island was slightly sheltered from the full force of the wind. Zac helped him lift out the mast and roll up the sail around the spars.

Out on its makeshift mooring the longboat was pitching and snatching at its anchor. Jake made a mental note to pull it ashore before they joined the others. But first they needed to lift *Privateer* up into the shelter of the trees. Meanwhile the other three, keeping together, hurried across to where they could see how *Moananui* was coping in the wind. What they saw made Tania's heart miss a beat.

Out in the anchorage the ketch was rearing like a bucking horse, yanking at her anchor-chain as vicious steep white-capped waves swept past her. Even while she was watching, Tania saw a flurry of wind lift a cloud of spray into the air. "Willywaws," she said, horrified. "We get them in New Zealand when the wind's over sixty knots! I hope the anchor doesn't drag." They could see both the twins' parents on deck. One was waving frantically

"The anchor's dragging!"

towards the direction of Jake's Jetty. The other – it looked like Mike – was at the stern doing something with the inflatable's painter. They saw the inflatable lift completely clear of the water and flip upside down. Just then the ketch began moving steadily backwards towards the rocky shore.

"Oh my god, the anchor's dragging!" shrieked Tania, panic stricken. "ZAC, JAKE, COME QUICK!" They began running back towards *Privateer* just as the pair of boys started sprinting towards them. As they met, the look on Tania's ashen face spoke for itself. While she blurted out what they had seen, all five of them set out at a run towards the jetty.

When they reached the fork in the trail, Zac broke away, leaving the other four to run the last few metres where they could be seen from the ketch. He sprinted back along the campsite track to the spot where he had flung down his sailbag full of clothing and gear only a short while earlier. Fumbling with the knot, he reached inside and felt for his coat. There in the pocket was the hand-held VHF. "Dammit," he muttered to himself, "still switched on!"

At a jog to rejoin the others, he could see Redbeard away to his left, out of the corner of his eye, sheltering behind a tree watching him. Without slowing down, Zac began calling *Moananui* over and over, but there was no response. As soon as he burst out of the scrub to the flat rock slab of Jake's Jetty he could see why. Out on the white ketch, partly obscured by driving spray and a squall of rain, he could make out his mother on the foredeck, winding in the anchor chain on the electric winch. His father was at the wheel and a flurry of churning water was boiling from the propeller under the stern. Even above the shriek of the gale he could hear the deep noise of a labouring diesel engine. Slowly *Moananui* was inching forward, rearing into the building waves.

Tania was still white. Jess looked as if she had the weight of the world on her shoulders. She was blaming herself for this crisis, and looked shattered. Jake was looking at the hand-held in Zac's hand. "What channel are you calling on?" he asked.

"I'll stay on seventy seven," answered Zac, and they could all see he was upset about something. "Trouble is," he admitted, "it's been left on all night and the battery warning light's on." He called again and saw his father calling out to Miriama who was just finishing settling the anchor into its chocks. She hurried back aft and disappeared into the cabin. Zac tried again. This time his mother's voice responded instantly, the strain evident in her tone, and no attempt at radio formalities.

"Zac we were dragging. We can't stay here. Don't even think of launching the dinghy in these conditions. Over."

"Hi Mum – we saw. We'll be okay here. We've got everything we need till you get back. Over." He deliberately didn't mention Redbeard and the gun.

"Zac you're very faint. We're going round to Apollo Bay. If it eases we'll come for you tonight, otherwise it'll have to be tomorrow. Are you all okay? Over."

"We're fine, you know we can all look after ourselves. Don't worry Mum. Over and out."

"So sorry, Zac – this is a disaster. Do take care. Love you both. Over and out."

As he listened Jake was torn between a feeling of horror and excitement. They were real castaways now. Marooned, with no escape possible until the gale blew out. And then, to add a new element of desperation, Jess gave out a yelp of disbelief.

"Look – the longboat!" Through the spray they could clearly make out the big white dinghy blowing backwards away from the island towards the Snake Bay shoreline. It seemed to be still attached to a rope and anchor which was preventing it from blowing sideways and tipping over. But it was obvious that the long endless line was no longer attached to the shore. Jake turned to Zac.

"What did you tie it to this morning?" he asked. Zac looked crestfallen.

"The tide was too far out to tie it to that log we used last night, so I just put some stones on top of the end. I didn't expect it to blow like this, ay," he explained, clearly mortified. "We should've pulled it in just now but when Tania screamed like that ..." He broke off and looked away. It was the closest Jess had seen him to tears. Seeing him that way stirred her back from her own private self-blame. We've got to get ourselves organised right now, she thought to herself. Again the Navy officer was stirring in Jess.

They were all nearly wet through. Fin was shivering, whether from shock or cold, she couldn't tell. Their bags were getting wet. She decided to take charge.

"Okay everyone this is what we're going to do," she announced firmly. To her surprise they all looked at her, waiting for orders. It was as if they had reached a state of mind where they all just needed someone to make decisions for them. "We're going to carry everything back to the clearing and set up the tents again," she said firmly. "The stuff needs to be covered up out of the rain squalls. We need to get dry clothes and raincoats on too. See, Fin's shivering. We'll stay together. I don't think Redbeard will be a problem. He needs shelter too. And mind out for dodgy trees – sometimes the branches come down in a gale like this."

Twenty minutes later, they had the two dome tents and the pup tent erected in a semi-circle near the edge of the campsite clearing, with the openings facing each other. The camp toilet was shifted into the bushes away to the east, so that the boys could all share the pup tent with the blue tarpaulin as a groundsheet. It was too windy to rig the sail as a shelter, so they had agreed to make the second dome tent into a food tent. Above them, the trees thrashed around as squall after squall of freezing rain swept overhead. Huddled together in the dome tent, reasonably dry again and pressed together for warmth, they discussed their situation.

Fin was first to speak. He had stopped shivering now. "I'm hungry," he declared. It was so typical of Fin that Jess couldn't stop herself from grinning. At least it meant the desperate edge of their situation had gone.

"Okay, after all it's nearly lunch time," she said. "It's a good thing we've got the twins' extra loaf. We could spread some stuff out in the food tent and take turns to dash in there to get sandwiches."

Next door the pup tent was flapping noisily. The bottom corners needed to be held down more securely. "We need to get some more stones around our tent," observed Jake. "Trouble is, we'll get soaked going all the way to the stone pile for them."

"Let's just pull out some of those bricks between squalls," suggested Zac. "Much easier."

Jess looked at her watch. She had just had a startling thought.

"Mum and Dad might still be trying to get here," she said, a hundred possibilities flooding into her mind. "I've got to go and look. Can anyone come with me? We've got to avoid doing things alone." There was not even a hesitation. Almost as a single person they all started to rise. Jake clutched his machete, and Fin had a fish knife in his hand.

From Stingray Rock, there was normally a good view right across the channel. But today they could barely make out the closest headland between the squalls. Sure enough, heeled right over in a cloud of spray, a little blue yacht was bravely battling the storm and approaching the reef cardinal mark. "They're triple reefed," exclaimed Jess. "No jib either. Probably motorsailing. Would've been a hell trip from Kettering!" Another rain squall swept over them and they did their best to shelter behind a large tree trunk. "Bugger Redbeard. We've got to let them see we're okay. I know they'll try coming in along the eastern side but there's no way they can anchor *Sea Fever* here in this! It'll be hard for them even to get out of the anchorage again if they come right in. *Sea Fever*'s engine is smaller than yours. Maybe we can get them now on your VHF, Zac."

Without a word, Zac handed her the VHF, pointing to the battery warning light. "Thanks," she said grimly, looking him directly in the eye with an acknowledgement of shared challenges. She flicked it to channel sixteen. "Worth a try," she murmured. "*Sea Fever, Sea Fever*, this is shore party, how copy, over." Silence except for the roar of a gale. "*Sea Fever*, this is shore party, how copy, over." Suddenly in a hiss of static came a response.

"Shore party this is *Sea Fever* go seven seven."

"Going up," said Jess, relief all over her face. She fiddled to switch it over to the talk channel and heard her mother's voice already calling.

"… party, this is *Sea Fever*. Are you there Jess, over."

"Mum this is Jess – we're okay here but you mustn't come in, over." Her mother's voice came back strained but clear.

"Jess you're very faint. It's really bad out here, are you sure you can wait till this eases? Over."

The VHF began to squeal in protest as Jess pushed the transmit button again. "Wait this gale out at Apollo Bay Mum, we are all okay. Over."

"I've almost lost you Jess. Think you said Apollo Bay. Over."

"WE ARE OKAY, OKAY," shouted Jess directly into the hand-held. She didn't even waste her breath saying over. They were all on Stingray Rock now, facing the wind and driving spray, waving as hard as they could.

"I heard you say okay, Jess. There's nothing we can do till this eases. You'll have to do your best, I know you will manage …" There was a brief pause, then an excited change of tone. "We can see you waving. Be careful, we'll be back as soon as it's safe. Over and out."

Moments later they were almost back at camp, cold and rather wet but feeling years older than ever before. Fin was at the front. Suddenly without any sound or warning he stopped dead in his tracks. They followed his gaze to see Redbeard standing in front of the tents.

Chapter 14

Stormy Explanations

THE FIRST THING JESS NOTICED, looking at Redbeard standing rather nervously near the tents, was that he was empty-handed. No gun, just a tall slightly hippy-looking character in a blue jacket, trying to call to someone in a tent over the noise of the thrashing trees overhead.

Jake took a firmer grip on his machete, and Fin tried to hold his fishing knife so that it looked menacing. Tania moved behind Zac. Then, as another heavy squall shook the trees above them and rain rattled against their coat hoods, they walked single file into the campsite. Redbeard was between them and the dome tents.

He had stopped calling now and was looking around curiously. Rainwater was running down his face as he turned his head towards the wind. As soon as he saw them grimly approaching with their machete and knife, his look changed to mild alarm. He raised both hands in a non-threatening gesture and began speaking loudly above the noise. The squall was passing now and the rain had been replaced by big droplets of water showering from the leaves as they shook overhead.

"Was that white dinghy yours?" he asked. "I came to tell you that it's blown away."

"Yeah, we saw that too, but we're okay," responded Jess cautiously, wondering how much information would be safe to give him.

"Are you kids here on your own in this weather?" he asked earnestly. Apart from his short beard his face was freckled, and from close up his eyes looked much softer than they expected. The others all looked towards Jess as if trusting her to be their unofficial spokesperson, and she hesitated. Should she admit that there were no adults anywhere to come to their aid? She looked into his face and took a snap decision. He looked like a decent person from this close. Not like the fat man of the other day.

"You'd better come into our tent out of the rain," she said. "We'll explain in there."

THE DOME TENT WAS designed for two people, not six. Jess remembered seeing a video of some shipwrecked people in a similar sized life-raft once. As they wriggled around to make space inside, she idly thought that this was almost like being in a life-raft during a storm. Except that at least this shelter wasn't bobbing around in the sea.

Fin was first to speak. He didn't mince his words. Certainly he wasn't going to easily forgive Redbeard for going through his tent yesterday. "Why did you try to burgle my tent?" he asked fiercely. He still had his knife handy in the pocket of his coat.

Redbeard looked puzzled. "I was only standing outside trying to call to anyone inside," he responded.

"I mean yesterday when you messed things up in my tent," continued Fin relentlessly.

Their visitor shook his head in genuine disbelief. "I would never go into anyone's tent unless it was an emergency," he insisted. "And yes I did see your tents yesterday, but I didn't come near them. Actually I was impressed with what responsible campers you seemed to be." A roar of wind shook the trees overhead as another squall swept across the island. Raindrops spattered loudly on the tent.

"Well someone ransacked it," continued Fin, now less certain of himself. "If it wasn't you, then who was it? We didn't think there was anyone else on the island yesterday."

Despite the need to explain their present circumstances, it was important that the matter of Fin's ransacking was cleared up, so the details began to come out. How the food supplies had been knocked over and the fishing sweatshirt interfered with ...

"Had you left the tent zipped up?" asked Redbeard knowingly. Fin squirmed uncomfortably.

"I think so ... I'm not sure, I was in a hurry." Jess threw him a dark look, and before either of them could speak, the stranger continued.

"I think I can explain your intruder. But first of all, tell me how come you're all here on your own in a storm like this?"

With the wind battering their tent and the roar of the waves breaking on the southern end of the island, the story of their marooning came out. Not methodically from start to end, but piecemeal, muddled up from five different viewpoints. In the end, their visitor interrupted, satisfied that he understood. "You're a pretty grown-up bunch of kids," he said. "I don't know how I would've coped at your age in this sort of crisis. And now I guess I'd better explain why I'm here." He paused and pulled out a battered map of the island, laminated in a plastic sleeve. Their mouths fell open when they saw what had been drawn onto it. Several large red crosses could be seen scattered randomly across the map.

Jake couldn't stop himself. "So you *are* after the treasure too!" He remembered the gun and went no further. Somehow this man didn't seem the sort who would kill for treasure.

"Treasure, what treasure?" asked the red-haired visitor. "No, this has nothing to do with anything as exciting as treasure. But it's still important and if the gale eases later you might even be able to help me. Anyway we haven't even introduced ourselves. I'm Rob, by the way. Perhaps you could all tell me your names and I'll try to remember them." As they introduced themselves one by one, he looked at each of them intently, clearly trying to memorise their names. He was particularly taken with Zac's name. "In the spirit of good old Aussie-Kiwi relations. That's a great name!"

"If you don't mind, Rob," interrupted Jess quickly and almost apologetically, "the rain's eased for a moment and we were going to grab a bite when we got back to camp. We could go and get ourselves a bit of food and eat it in here while you tell us your side of the story." Rob pulled out a muesli bar and drink bottle while they took turns to rush into the food tent. Outside it was still wild. It seemed amazing how such a flimsy wall of fabric could seem to provide such a protective shelter from the elements.

"Has anyone heard of the forty-spotted pardalote?" Rob began unexpectedly as the last young body wriggled back into the tent. Baffled, Zac responded instantly.

"Sounds like some sort of butterfly."

"It's a small bird isn't it?" Jake cut in.

"Actually it's the most endangered bird in Australia, and it

Forty-spotted pardalote

lives here," continued Rob. "The only two significant colonies left are on Bruny and Maria Islands, and the breeding pairs here on Snake Island are a vital part of the Bruny ones. Snake Island is predator-free, you see – or at least it should be."

Until now Fin had been looking at the red-head blankly, wondering if he was trying to sidestep the explanation about his tent burglary. But as Rob began talking of Snake Island having special significance he began to show interest.

"What's predator-free?" he interrupted, speaking louder than normal to be heard over another squall, and treating Rob with less suspicion than earlier.

"It means free of hunting animals like rats and foxes," Jess butted in equally loudly, anxious to show that she knew what Rob was talking about.

"Or, in this case, feral cats," added Rob. "They're the most advanced and dangerous threat to tree-nesting birds around here, with their retractable claws and razor sharp teeth. Cats and loss of habitat are the two biggest reasons for the near extinction of the forty-spotted."

"What habitat?" This time it was Zac interrupting.

"*Eucalyptus viminalis* – more commonly called the white gum," said Rob instantly. "It's the only tree the forty-spots will live in or even nest in. They eat its special sap as well as the insects that live in it. The trouble is that so many of these trees have been destroyed by forestry, and the birds won't travel very far between clusters of white gums. The trees around this clearing are white gums so you might've noticed some of the birds. They're really small."

"We've watched some tiny ones that flitter around like butterflies," said Jess eagerly.

"Sounds like forty-spots all right. They're so quick that it's hard to photograph them."

They were all listening intently, but Fin wasn't going to let

Rob ignore the subject of his burglary. "You said you'd tell us who broke into my tent," he cut in, before anyone else could ask irrelevant questions. As he spoke, there was a sudden loud crack from somewhere near outside – much louder than another one they had noticed earlier. Startled, they turned, as Jake unzipped the door and peered around.

"That branch came down like Dad said it might," he announced, and explained to the others about how the toilet tent had been under a cracked tree. After they had settled back down, their red-bearded visitor returned to the subject of Fin's ransacked tent.

"Well firstly I don't think you zipped it properly up, Fin, and secondly I think your intruder was more interested in fish than maps," he said. "Has anyone noticed any animal droppings or heard animal noises at night?" Jake and Jess both spoke up, mentioning the scratching noises and droppings. Jess also remembered how some water had disappeared from pots on two occasions.

"Something kept pinching my bait too," added Fin.

"Okay," continued Rob. "I paddled over here yesterday to check on my birds – they're almost like my own kids these ones. I visit them whenever I can. And there were five separate cat droppings around the island. It can't have been here for more than ten days because I would've noticed any droppings when I was here last. It's definitely a cat – probably feral – and how it got here nobody knows! I shudder to think how many birds it's killed already. Say, surely you didn't bring it over did you?"

"No way!" said Jess and Jake almost in unison. They were all beginning to understand how far from reality their crazy misunderstandings had been.

"Okay I get it," said Zac. "The cat got into Fin's open tent looking for food and drink, ay. And it must be feral or it would've been all over us, expecting cuddles and saucers of milk."

"Right. So I hope I'm off the hook," said Redbeard with mock fierceness. "I must admit I found the idea of having to share my island with a mob of kids a bit challenging at first."

"We did notice you were avoiding us," said Jake. "So I guess the crosses on your map are about nesting sites are they?"

"Right," he replied. "And at this very moment there's a wet cat somewhere out there, thinking about which tasty bird or lizard he's going to have for dinner when the wind dies down. I've set a trap for him in case he gets hungry. With a nice piece of fresh fish inside. But if I have to, I'll shoot him. He wouldn't live long on this island in a dry summer anyway, but he may live long enough to eat all my birds." He looked almost tearful. The tent was shaking again and outside the pup tent was flapping wildly, but nobody even noticed the din. They were all watching him and thinking.

"Does Captain Bligh help you count the birds?" asked Fin suddenly. Redbeard looked baffled, so Jess interpreted for him.

"He means the grey haired man who ferried you over this morning."

"Oh, that's Alan Woodrupp. He's mad keen about this island too. He helped get it listed as a state reserve. He told me you were lighting fires but I told him that it didn't seem likely from what I'd seen of how well you were managing your camp. Minimum impact, excellent work. It's what I like to see in a campsite."

"He said I caught undersized fish," broke in Fin, "but I didn't. I always measure them and put the tiddlers back in carefully." He was getting wound up again, and Jess interrupted him.

"The fire was lit by a pair of men in a tinny. They were horrible ..." She paused briefly, her face reddening. "It started to spread but we managed to put it out." He was looking at her intently, and his expression showed that he believed her. Relieved, she continued. "We heard them another time in the middle of the night, climbing onto the fish-farm ..." Again she hesitated, realising too late that she had broken the pledge to keep their midnight adventure secret. But their redhaired visitor was sitting bolt upright, fully focussed on what she had said.

"Onto the fish farm! In the dark? Are you sure?"

"We were out fishing on the reef. But you mustn't tell our parents. It was definitely them, we could hear them talking about seeing us that day. There was a big boat near the shore and they were going backwards and forwards to the pens." She stopped, aware that she was babbling too fast, like her little brother.

"Did they have any registration number on their boat?" he asked intently.

"Probably but I didn't notice. There were a couple of stickers on it. You know the sort, 'Kill Ferals' and 'Greens tell lies'. One was quite fat ..."

"I got a picture of them on Jess's mobile," interrupted Fin. "But the battery's flat now."

"Well after we get over this storm, I'd really like to get more details from you on those men. I know somebody who'll be very interested in what you saw."

Outside, the rain squalls were becoming less frequent, though the wind was continuing to roar in the trees around them. The noise of breaking waves was even louder than it had been when they were watching *Sea Fever*. Rob looked at his watch and raised himself to as near a standing position as the cramped tent would allow.

"Mid-afternoon already! Doesn't look like this is going to blow itself out till morning. My tent's back near your black dinghy. I'm going to check the trap now. I might need to borrow a fish head, Fin, if that cat escapes with my bait." He unzipped the tent and pulled up his blue hood. "I'll call in a bit later to see how you're all going." And he was off.

Chapter 15

Blood is Spilt

WITH REDBEARD GONE, THE TENT seemed suddenly much bigger. They were aware of small puddles of water on the floor, partly brought in on their wet coats, and partly from the drips which had come in from the tent seams above their heads. They began to think of the discomfort ahead of them, the remaining hours of stormy daylight and a cold night in wet tents.

"Let's play cards," suggested Tania. "It's one way we can fill in time till dinner." It seemed like a good idea and there was a general discussion about which game to play. Eventually they decided to start with 'Cheat' and later teach each other some favourites.

But first they needed to do something about the pup tent which had flogged itself so loose that the boys' gear had become quite wet during the rain squalls. Zac and Fin set to work tightening the guy-ropes and re-arranging the groundsheet. Jake began pulling up the bricks from the patch they had discovered the previous day, to use as weights around the side-flaps. As he levered them out with his shovel, he noticed that the rusty pipe underneath was attached to some sort of rusty mechanism and rotten wood.

There was something familiar about his find. He had seen a thing like this before in a museum. "Hey Zac," he called excitedly, "this looks like some sort of rusty old gun!"

Zac was beside him in a flash. "It's pretty old, ay," he agreed. "That bit looks like some sort of lever on top, and that's definitely a trigger there. Let's dig it up."

But Jake wasn't so sure. It could easily fall apart if they weren't careful. "No I think we'll just leave it alone for now. We could ask Redbeard – Rob – what he thinks we should do with it." It had been his find, and he felt personally responsible for it. The tent was still flapping so they set to work weighing down the edges with bricks until it had been tamed. The others all came to see Jake's find when he told them about it, and Jess agreed with Jake.

"I wonder how old it is?" she pondered. "It might be an old musket. Someone probably hid it under those bricks wrapped up in a sack or something."

"We think those bricks were the hearth of the fireplace in that family's house," added Jake. "Maybe this is the gun those convicts used when they invaded the island!" They looked with much greater interest at the rusty relic now. "I'm going to tell the museum about it, after the holidays," Jake continued. "It might not be treasure but it's still something interesting." He covered it with one of the boards they had found during their expedition yesterday. Funny, it seemed so long ago that they had been happily beachcombing on a sunny beach.

Once the tent had been tamed, Jess suggested a quick look at the anchorage. Sitting in the tent had cramped their legs and it was good to see what was happening outside the campsite. The wind was still howling but there were quite long periods between rain squalls now. Wet grass quickly saturated their feet and legs as they walked fast along the track to Jake's Jetty.

It was immediately obvious that no boat would survive in the anchorage area where *Moananui* had been a few hours earlier. The waves were much longer and higher now, occasionally breaking as they swept past the eastern side of the island. The wind had settled in to a steady gale but at least there were no more of Tania's williwaws lifting spray high into the air. Without anyone saying it, they all knew that they were definitely going to be marooned on the island tonight.

"Let's go and play cards," said Fin, and they hurried back to the shelter of the girls' tent for a few hours of distraction.

PLAYING CARDS IS a great way to pass time, and by the time they had played a few rounds of 'Cheat', followed by several more of 'Hearts', it was nearly dinner time and they were quite stiff from being squeezed up in the tiny tent. It was still noisy outside but they were so used to it by now that they hardly noticed the roaring. Several times they had heard the crack of falling branches from further down the island.

They began to discuss what to eat for dinner. Zac and Tania had no food left, but as their big pie had fed everyone last night, the original castaways still had plenty of food in their store. Jess started looking through the cans, deciding what combination to use.

"I wonder what sort of food Rob's cooking up?" said Tania, remembering that he had said he would be back.

"Perhaps we should see if he wants to come and eat here with us," suggested Jess. So they decided to all take a walk to the south end and check if *Privateer* was still all right, as well as visiting Rob's camp.

Jake's little pirate ship was no longer the brand new looking dinghy it had been a few days earlier. There were some visible scratches along the black sides from various incidents involving oysters and rocks which Jake ruefully told himself could not really be helped. Quite a lot of rainwater had collected in the bottom, along with a surprising number of leaves and twigs floating about. They all helped empty it out and leave it upside down. Jake tried to ignore the scratches on the bottom. "Pirate ships always had scrapes from reefs during storms," he told the others, thinking of how he would sand down and repaint his beautiful boat once their holidays were over.

They could see Rob's low narrow yellow tent under the trees not far from *Privateer*. It was a tunnel tent, the type used by mountaineers with barely enough room for a sleeping bag. They called out to him as soon as they reached it but there was no response.

"He's probably out hunting for the cat," said Fin. "Let's go and look for him."

"Okay but we'll need to go quietly in case we scare it," warned Jake. Splitting into two groups, they began their search. The three boys walked along the east side while Tania and Jess tried the west side. The route the girls had chosen had thicker scrub so their progress was slower and wetter than on the more well-worn trail that the boys had taken.

For the boys, the track to Stingray Rock showed no sign of the red-bearded cat hunter. The rock was being lashed by breaking waves and the trees were thrashing about quite a lot more than at the north end of the island. None of them wanted to stay there long, so they decided to continue tracking clockwise around the island to meet the girls.

They were not far along the western side when Fin heard a wailing noise over the din of wind and waves. It didn't take long to find where the noise was coming from. It was a cage with one very angry tabby cat inside. As soon as they approached, it began hurling itself at the bars hissing and screeching. They all backed off.

"I wonder where Rob's got to?" said Jake, and they stood about for a few moments wondering whether to check back at camp in case he was there already, or to wait near the trapped cat for the girls.

At that very same moment, the girl search party was barely thirty metres away, searching much more thoroughly than the boys had been. Tania was looking carefully to her right, while Jess was a few metres inland looking to her left towards the middle of the island. The scrub was quite thick on this side and they had realised that they would easily miss Rob if he was crouching in the scrub looking for cat tracks.

"Over there, Tania!" Jess could see a scrap of blue up near a rise to her left. It was worth checking. They could see where a large branch had come down from a high tree up near the rise, and automatically looked up in case there were any other branches poised to fall on their heads. Approaching the blue object, Jess suddenly realised to her horror what it was. She broke into a run and behind her, Tania, sensing her urgency, began running too.

Rob, when they reached him, was lying face down with a heavy broken branch across his back. Alongside him was a small bag and his gun. He was not moving. The branch was heavy but they managed to lift it off before kneeling to see if he was still alive.

"Have you done any First Aid courses?" Jess asked Tania urgently, her heart in her mouth. Tania nodded.

"Only a basic one though."

"Me too, what do we do first?" They looked at each other briefly, desperately aware that they probably needed to act fast. "*Doctors ABC,*" continued Jess. "What do those letters stand for? D for Danger, something starting with R, then S, S...?"

"Send for help," offered Tania.

"Can't, my phone's dead!" said Jess wryly. "Airway, Breathing ..."

"Compression," Tania completed it for her. "At least the danger's probably gone now that branch is down." By now they were kneeling on either side of his head, neither of them quite sure about touching his face with its freckles and short beard. They had never been quite so close to a man before except their fathers, which was quite different. But just as Jess plucked up courage to grasp his head and feel for his breath, he stirred and groaned. His eyes were still shut. Tania reached his wrist to begin feeling for his pulse. As she fumbled with his jacket sleeve he became aware of the girls and opened his eyes. His hand was very cold, she noticed, as he began to speak.

"Is he breathing?"

He spoke softly and was clearly in pain. "It landed on my left shoulder," he said, wincing. "Something's broken, but at least it missed my head." His teeth were chattering now and there was blood on his face. "What's the time?" he asked, after trying to look at his watch and groaning in agony.

"Half past five," said Jess and saw him react in surprise.

"I must've been here for a couple of hours then." He lapsed into silence. "Say, you don't have any painkillers do you?"

"We've got a basic First Aid kit. There are painkillers and I think there's a thermo-blanket in it too." Jess's mind was working overtime. Should she give him anything to eat or drink? Could they move him? Should he be in hospital, and if so how quickly? She turned to Tania. "We've got to find the others. Do you want to stay with him or shall I?" They both stood up. Jess moved a few paces away, turned around to avoid alarming him, and yelled as loudly as possible towards the south of the island. To her great relief there was an answering yell over the noise of the wind.

It didn't take long for the boys to find them. In the meantime Rob had managed to set her mind to rest about some of her uncertainties. He was clearly in agony but was sure his head was all right except for a long clotted scratch down his left cheek. His left shoulder and arm were badly hurt, and he wasn't sure if he had injured his back. Certainly it hurt to move. At least he knew about First Aid, so could help them make decisions.

As soon as the others had arrived Jess set some things in action. "He's badly hurt," she said, sounding more confident than she felt. "Tania, can you stay here while the rest of us get some things from camp?" Jess's mind was working overtime. They should shift all the tents onto that rise before dark. And they should bring his sleeping bag and spare clothes too. She wished she knew whether they could let him have any food. She knew that people going into hospital shouldn't be fed. But it was impossible to get him to hospital anyway. Perhaps he had a radio or phone.

"Jacket pocket …" He mumbled faintly when she asked him. It felt wrong to be feeling around in a man's pocket, but Jess found his mobile quickly enough. The pocket was very wet and the phone was clearly soaked. After a couple of minutes she gave up trying to turn it on and turned her attention back to organising the camp shift.

"We'll be back as soon as we can, Rob, and we should be able to warm you up soon." At least she had spent enough time surveying the island to realise that their camp was only a short distance inland through the scrub. In fact she was sure that she could see a clear patch in the tree canopy not far ahead.

As they hurried off she explained what she wanted to happen. "We can't move him to our camp," she said firmly. "His back could be broken and he's cold, so we have to move the camp to him. We've got to get him under shelter and warmed up. He's been there for a couple of hours already. Zac could you and Jake get the sail bundled up so we can make a bivvy for him. Fin, move the stuff from your tent into the food tent so we can use the blue ground-sheet for shelter too. I'm getting the First Aid kit and cooker with a pot of water."

"We should mark a bit of a track now so we can find our way back more easily," suggested Zac, scuffing the ground and moving a branch to point in the right direction.

Jess was right about how close the camp was, and they set to work as quickly as possible. It took only a few minutes to gather up everything she had asked for and they set off back to the accident site. It wasn't too hard to follow the route they had already used, but they stopped and moved a few extra branches to help mark it better for the next trips.

Tania looked relieved to see them so quickly. "He's getting really cold!" she said as soon as they returned. Jess gave him two Panadol which he swallowed sleepily. She tried to remember what the warning signs of delayed shock and hypothermia were, as she and Zac carefully tucked the shiny thermal blanket around him and began rigging the sail over him for a shelter. Tania was heating some water on the stove while Jake and Fin rushed off to get Rob's gear from his tent.

"We've got to stop him from going to sleep," Tania told them and they took turns to talk to him.

"I knew it would be bad weather but it was the only break I had from work for trapping the cat," he explained groggily. At least the pills were helping ease the pain. When Zac told him about the cat in the cage they all sensed his relief, and he brightened noticeably. "Well at least this pain isn't for nothing," he murmured through clenched teeth.

Before long Jake and Fin were back with Rob's gear and they unzipped his sleeping bag to cover him up. They debated whether to take off his wet jeans but no-one was confident enough to do it. Instead they gave him a soft-drink bottle full of hot water to hug. "At least it'll help keep up his body temperature," said Jess. Then they decided to bring the rest of the camp to be as near to Rob as possible. The pills had helped but he was drifting in and out of consciousness and they were all getting worried. What if his injuries were worse than he was letting on?

Finally Jake made his mind up. He had been thinking about it for some time and knew that the others must have considered it too. Up until now it had been Jess and Tania who seemed to have been making the decisions, but now it was time for him to make a vital announcement.

"I'm going sailing!" he stated. "We've got to get help before dark!"

Chapter 16

Desperate Voyage

JAKE WAS ABSOLUTELY SERIOUS ABOUT his proposal to sail to Captain Bligh's shack. He knew that Jess would be against it, but he had studied the wave patterns when he and Fin had gone for Redbeard's gear. There was definitely a calmer patch between the island and the stony beach of Snake Bay, where the waves were in the wind shadow of the island. If he could only stay in this corridor of calmer sea, he might be able to sail across without capsizing. His first hurdle was to convince Jess.

It was the first time he had ever seen her so stressed. She knew how desperately they needed to get help for Rob, but on the other hand, how could she possibly agree to letting Jake risk his life? And Jake knew that she could still physically stop him. It was not just a case of her saying no. She could stop him from ever getting *Privateer* into the water by holding onto the boat or even hiding his rudder and sails under a bush somewhere. He had to actually convince her that he could do it safely. And there wasn't too much time until it would begin getting dark.

The best way to convince her was to take her to the northern end of the island and show her what his plan was. So while Zac and Tania began cooking up a dinner of canned stew and tomatoes, they walked back to the gravel beach just past Rob's tent. On both sides of the island the white-capped waves were still sweeping past, but she had to agree that it seemed quieter directly to the north. However it was not a parallel-sided rectangle of calm. The waves wrapped around the island and nearly joined up by the time they met the Snake Bay shoreline. And there was clearly plenty of wind hitting the water from about halfway across, where there was no protection from the trees on the island. They walked back to the new campsite in silence as Jess battled with her internal conflict.

They were nearly there when Jess said something which let Jake know what her decision was. "Remember that solar light we found at Flotsam Beach? I saw it flashing orange last night. It wasn't broken after all. It must automatically switch itself on at night. So if we leave it on the beach, your rescue party could use it as a lighthouse to find their way here in the dark. But you'll have to make it over before dark." Jake would have hugged her but it was far too serious a trip to think about hugs. The next fifteen minutes were spent thinking about how best to reduce the risks.

Rob was barely conscious now, but he was able to understand what Jake was intending to do. "Go straight to Alan Woodrupp's," he murmured, breathing raggedly. "He'll know what's best to do. But don't drown or I'll never forgive myself!"

Tania insisted on Jake eating bread and stew even though it was not fully heated. Jess gave him a bar of chocolate which she had been keeping for emergencies. There were so many risks, not just drowning. They ran through the obvious ones while he was eating.

"It's nearly low tide so the oysters could be a problem," said Jess, remembering how once Fin had sliced his foot badly on a razor-sharp oyster shell and needed stitching up. "You'll just have to wear your sneakers and get them wet." Tania began to fuss then about the cold. She was still concerned with how cold Rob had been when they found him.

"Put on my spare sweatshirt over yours. The lifejacket over your coat will help too. Also keep your hood up. A woollen hat would be better but there aren't any here."

"There's one in my pack," murmured Rob, still sufficiently aware of the plans to respond. "And some gloves." Tania rummaged through and found them.

"We'll need the torches here so you'll have to get help before dark, ay. No point ruining a good torch getting it wet anyway," added Zac. They hurried off to *Privateer*'s resting place, aware of the approaching nightfall, leaving Tania to heat another bottle for Rob.

Jake had thought hard already about how best to rig *Privateer*. At first he had considered just rowing across, jollyboat fashion. But when he remembered how hard it had been to row straight with the Optimist's flat bottom and no keel, he realised that it would be too dangerous. It was blowing hard near the other side even though the waves were not big in the narrow sheltered strip. If he couldn't control his direction he could easily be pushed out of the safest waters into the waves and then spun sideways. That would almost definitely tip him over. No, he decided, I'll have to rig the rudder and sail her over.

He thought about his sailing lessons, and how he could reduce the sail area. By sailing without a sprit he would keep the size down by half. It might not be very good for the sail but this was an emergency. Working together they stepped the mast and he folded the sail over, with the peak loosely tied down to the boom to stop it flapping. The four of them carried the little black boat across the stones down to the water's edge. It seemed a long way with the tide so far out.

Eddies of wind from several directions were swinging the sail around wildly. They waded out until it was deep enough for him to fix the rudder in place and slide the centreboard part way down in its slot. He felt like an astronaut preparing for a space launching under his bulky clothes and lifejacket. Three pairs of eyes watched his face closely as he threaded the mainsheet through its blocks and began to pull it in. He had automatically begun to tie a figure of eight knot in the end but at the last minute he stopped himself. Instinctively it seemed better to be able to let everything go if necessary.

Normally he would have given a piratical gesture as he sailed away, but instead he sat down in the bottom, leaned back and gave a thumbs up. "Blast-off," he yelled and they pushed him out towards the wind.

From the island, three castaways watched him anxiously. The light was beginning to fade, and they began moving restlessly as *Privateer* drifted slowly away with its stumpy little triangle of sail flipping from one side to the other.

"He'd better sail faster than that or he'll still be floundering around when it's dark," said Zac, reflecting how they all felt. The situation was so urgent and yet the rescue mission seemed so slow. And then, suddenly, they heard a squall rushing through the trees behind them, swooping down onto the water between them and Jake. They saw the little black boat surge ahead and rush off in a flurry of white water, rapidly disappearing towards the distant shore. In a moment the red sail was totally hidden behind a cloud of spray and rain, and nothing further could be seen.

After five minutes Jess broke the silence. "We can't all stay here and leave Tania holding the fort. I'll stay and watch till it clears and you two should go back to help. We have to bring the last load from the old campsite before dark and get the tents up. Just the dome tents will do. And we can't leave that cat in its cage without water or something. I'll be back as soon as I've seen Jake again." Zac looked at her to say something, but

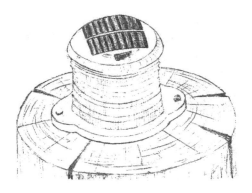

Jess's lighthouse

changed his mind when he saw the tormented look on her face. He would normally have insisted on staying too, but now it was best not to argue.

"Okay Jess," he said. "Get back as soon as you can, ay. Let's go Fin." Before she knew it, Jess was alone.

Ten minutes later, the Snake Bay shore was just visible again. Jess could make out a black shape high on the beach, possibly *Privateer*. There was no sign of anyone moving. It was not what she had wanted to see. Perhaps Jake had capsized and the boat washed up by itself. Feeling even more helpless, she set the solar light down on a stump near where they had rigged *Privateer*. Then, casting one last look across the water, she strode off back to the new campsite. 'Camp Disaster' she would name it. There was nothing more she could do here.

FOR WEEKS AFTERWARDS, Jake remembered every detail of that desperate voyage. His biggest impression was how lonely he felt. There was so much at stake and so little that anyone could do to help him while he was on the water. For an outsider

139

it would seem that his maiden voyage across the channel from Kettering would have been far more memorable. After all, this trip was only about half a kilometre in distance. But the circumstances were so different.

After he was first pushed off, the problem, surprisingly, was lack of wind. There was only a slight joggle of wavelets lapping on either side of the boat, coming off the edge of the huge whitecaps roaring past only fifty metres away on either side. The wind was fitful, puffing first from one direction then the other, and a couple of times even from ahead. He knew that this was because of the eddies of air curling into the wind-shadow of the trees like swirls of water behind logs in a river. Then just ahead he could see dark riffles on the sea surface, and suddenly a violent squall of wind caught his sail from directly behind and he was away in a cloud of rain and spray.

He had never sailed so fast in his life, even though it was only a tiny sail area. He wondered whether to sit up on the side of the boat but decided that his weight would be better where he was, crouching in the middle. It was like a wild sleigh ride with the bow-wave creaming down both sides of the boat. The air was full of flying spray as he clutched the tiller and focussed on steering for the only part of the shore which didn't seem to have giant waves breaking onto it. On his starboard side he could see someone running towards the same place, but he dared not look in case he lost concentration on his steering.

He felt the growing waves pick up the stern of the boat and he knew he was surfing. If he was to lose control at this stage, the boat would be upside-down in a flash and it would be a disaster. At any moment now he could be hurled onto the terrible stones and oysters, slicing him and his precious boat to pieces.

"LET GO THE MAINSHEET!" a voice yelled over the roar of waves and wind. It was Captain Bligh, up to his waist in swirling water only a few metres ahead. Jake let the rope

... he knew he was surfing

run free, and immediately the sail swivelled around the mast,
flapping freely like a flag as the boat slowed down. A powerful
hand clutched the side of the boat and drew him towards the
shore as he pulled up the centreboard and rudder and leapt over
the side to help. Wordlessly he and the grey haired man lifted
Privateer up the stony beach clear of the water and set her down.
Captain Bligh looked at him, his eyes obviously expecting an
explanation for this crazy stunt.

"I had to do it," said Jake urgently. "It's an emergency. We
have to get Rob to hospital."

Chapter 17

Captain Bligh does his Bit

FOR A MAN THEY HAD thought was old and rather deaf, Captain Bligh was remarkably capable and fit. In fact Jake very quickly changed his opinion of this rather grim character they had all disliked since the fire. For a start he was not particularly old, maybe in his late fifties. But his face was weather-beaten, and Jake sensed a sadness in his eyes.

Jake was exhausted from the nervous tension of the last few hours. It was an enormous relief to have someone strong to take over the rescue now – strong both physically and mentally. It was as if this man could see right inside him to read his mind and feel his tension. As soon as Jake had poured out the reasons for his wild ride across from the island, his rescuer reached over and shook his hand. It seemed a strange thing to do as it was happening, but when Jake grasped that firm brown hand in response, it became clear that their relationship had instantly changed. This was a gesture of recognition, of mutual respect. They faced each other as fellow beings in a crisis, and Jake knew that everything would be all right now.

"I'm Alan Woodrupp," said the man loudly above the noise of the storm. "And you're a very brave young man."

"I'm Jake Brownrig," responded Jake equally loudly, shivering slightly. "And by the way, we didn't light that fire."

"I realise that now," said Alan. He wasn't a man to talk much. "Let's get your boat de-rigged up near the bank, then we can get things moving." The place where Jake had steered ashore had been used before for boat launchings, he could see. The oysters and large rocks had been cleared away leaving a wide strip of stony beach. Up on the bank were several boats. An old varnished clinker dinghy, an aluminium punt and a white dinghy. As they neared the bank, Jake jerked with surprise. It was their longboat up there with Captain Bligh's boats.

Alan noticed his reaction. "That's your other boat isn't it? I saw it dragging this way. A mighty long anchor rope you were using! It's safe here for now." Jake mumbled his thanks and a brief explanation of why it had drifted away, but he wasn't sure if the older man could hear. By now they were walking fast towards Captain Bligh's shack. Tall spindly trees were bending in the wind overhead and the track was muddy.

The shack was a small two-roomed cottage, its outside walls clad in weathered planks. A shed nearby was full of firewood, and had a yellow plywood sailing dinghy suspended under the roof. Alan wiped his feet and strode in through the front door, flicking on a light switch. "Leave your shoes on," he said. "I can clean up later. We've got to work fast. The kettle's over there, boil up some water would you."

He disappeared into the second room briefly and came out in a dry pair of trousers. Then he went straight to the phone and dialled a number. Jake listened to his side of the conversation. It was obviously a policeman on the other end, and equally obvious that Alan knew him well. Wind speeds were discussed – something about a fifty knot limit for helicopters. Stretcher type, paramedic availability. Every now and then, he would ask Jake for a detail about Rob's injuries. "Unspecified upper-body internal injuries," Jake heard Alan say. "Certainly broken bones in the left shoulder area. The lad says he's struggling to stay conscious. We've got to move fast."

From the way he talked, Jake knew they had under-estimated Captain Bligh. He had an air of authority about him, and Jake wondered if he had been in the police force or army. He saw Alan pause and unfold a map. Then he read a set of co-ordinates over the phone. Jake thought of something and waved urgently to interrupt him.

"There's an orange flashing light at the beach where we launched. It's near the flat area where that fire was. It might help a rescue party." Alan nodded in a grateful gesture, and relayed the information to the unseen policeman, finishing the conversation by giving his own mobile number.

"I'm going to try to get out there now, myself," he said. "Thanks, Mick. I'll get back with any developments." He hung up and looked out the window. It was nearly dark. "Are you up for a wild ride back?" he asked. "It'll be wet but we can make it there." Jake nodded, his eyes gleaming. He felt helpless here in this small house. Getting back to the island would be the best thing possible, especially with a man like this who seemed to know so much about search and rescue.

Alan insisted that they eat a sandwich and have a quick hot drink. He was pulling on some wet-weather trousers and a coat as he ate. Then he disappeared briefly and returned with a waterproof bag. "Dry clothes for you when we get there," he explained briefly. "They were my son's but he doesn't need them any more ..." He broke off in silence and looked away. Jake sensed that same sadness he had first noticed in the man.

With no further ado, Alan picked up two waterproof torches, tossed one to Jake and strode out the door, leaving the light on. "Let's go."

IT WAS GETTING dark at Camp Disaster and Jess was in a state of high stress. She had such a burden of responsibility and guilt that she was finding it difficult to function. Zac and Tania could sense this in her, and being twins, they didn't need to say much. Instead they quietly took control. When Jess had returned to camp in a state of near hysteria, half an hour earlier, Tania had put her arms around her and reassured her that things were under control. Zac had put his hand on her arm too in a meaningful male gesture that had somehow drawn some of the tension out of her body. Fin responded to the Kiwi twins' leadership without any questioning. As long as someone seemed to be in control he was happy to cooperate.

Tania eased Jess into the cooking activities, feeling that it would give her something to take her mind off all the uncertainties. Rob was asleep now, or unconscious, and they took turns to check his pulse and breathing. His chest rose and fell in a steady rhythm and he had stopped groaning. To Tania's relief he seemed to have warmed up again with a sleeping bag tucked around him and two drink bottles full of hot water next to his body. The scratch on his face was not too deep and she had left it alone for now, just wiping the dried blood off his cheek. She idly wondered whether she should train as a medic when she left school.

Zac was enjoying setting up the new camp with Fin. He had his own way of doing things and it was good to be able to do them his way instead of Jake's. The last camp had been Jake's because he and Tania were the late-comers. But this one had become his own. He had even brought Jess's stinkapotty and rigged the pup tent over it, away to the north a few paces. They had put the cat near it, still snarling in its cage. He had managed to give it some water.

Jess had decided to add another course to the basic meal of stew and bread which they had already eaten. She had opened two tins of fruit and cooked them up with flour dumplings on top. She thought that lots of warm carbohydrates would do them good. As she cooked with her head-torch shining in the pot, she realised that the storm noises were definitely less than before. The wind had eased below gale force now, she was sure, and there had been no rain since she had returned from watching Jake.

She had just decided that it might be worth walking back to check if the orange light was flashing when there was a flicker of torchlight from the track, and Jake walked purposefully into camp clutching a bag, closely followed by Captain Bligh. Both were dripping wet. Everyone began talking at once, but the older man interrupted.

"You've done a great job here I can see," he said. "Now I need to look at Rob." He was stripping off his dripping wet-weather gear as he spoke. They watched as he knelt, Tania briefly explaining the most important details about his change in breathing patterns and temperature. Rob stirred and groaned as the older man shone a light onto his face and began asking questions. Alan lifted the sleeping bag off his legs and poked each one. He seemed pleased when Rob told him he could feel them both.

"So far so good," he said, and began talking to Rob, asking questions clearly designed to find out how good his memory was. The five castaways watched and listened, fascinated. They were all rapidly changing their minds about this man they had disliked so much before.

"We came back in his punt," said Jake excitedly. "The aluminium one with the outboard. It was a wicked ride." He described how expertly Alan had driven the flat-bottomed punt into the wind, how he varied the throttle for the waves, and how he seemed to know exactly where the calmer water was, even in the near darkness. "That flashing light makes an awesome lighthouse. The chopper should be here soon."

During the pause they could hear Rob telling Alan about the black-shirts and the fire, and how they had been seen at the salmon farm. Alan swivelled his head to look at them. He looked quite different from how Jess and Fin remembered him when his face had been flushed with anger at the fire. Now he looked at them with obvious respect and a curious wistfulness. "I misjudged you kids," he said, "and I'm sorry."

"I always put the tiddlers back," said Fin.

"I'm sure you do," he replied.

THE HELICOPTER, WHEN it came half an hour later, completely drowned out the sound of the wind. They knew it was coming soon because Alan's mobile had rung. "I need three of you to come with me," he had said after a very brief phone conversation. "Tania, would you mind staying with Rob. You seem to be a good nurse. Who can stay with her?" No-one had spoken at first, all wanting to see the helicopter landing, so Jess had offered to stay. After all, Tania would be missing out too, and they would all be able to see it take off later.

Even from the camp its crackling throbbing rotor blades made conversation nearly impossible. Rob was thoroughly awake and his face was alive with relief. "You kids deserve a medal," he said.

Meanwhile, at the gently sloping open grassy area near the black-shirts' fireplace, Alan had positioned the three boys just under the trees with torches. "Don't move from there," he ordered sternly. "Shine them on the ground over there and cover your eyes when it gets near the ground." It was almost unnecessary, as a blinding searchlight suddenly beamed down onto the landing area. Alan waved to indicate the best landing spot and gave the thumbs up before running back to join the boys. Slowly the helicopter began to float down towards the ground, wobbling a little as a gust hit it, and hovering briefly just above the grass before settling its runners firmly down.

Once it was safe, the pilot and a woman climbed down, bringing a heavy bag and an orange hard plastic scoop stretcher. Alan pointed to the boys. "They can bring the stretcher. Is there anything else we need?" A box was lifted out and then Alan asked Jake to lead the way back to camp. He knew the way so well now that he could almost do it blindfolded.

Tania was thrilled to be so closely involved in such an intense medical emergency. The woman asked her and Jess some unexpected questions about the weight and height of the tree branch, and about how Rob had seemed when they first found him. It all seemed so professional, the way they handled him as they took his temperature and asked him questions. The man talked for a while to Alan about moving the stretcher while the lady paramedic gave him an injection and explained carefully to him how he was going to be flown to hospital in Hobart. Rob seemed groggy but calm, and certainly relieved.

Tania and Jess were instructed how to help lift Rob onto the stretcher while Alan told the boys what he wanted them to do. "We need enough light so nobody trips over," he said. "Jake I want you in front again with the big torch up high shining downwards. Fin you need to follow us with another torch. The rest of us will carry the stretcher."

With three on each side, the stretcher didn't seem too heavy. Alan had obviously done this before, and he talked to them all to keep them in step, or to move left or right when needed. It didn't take long to have Rob loaded into the helicopter for his flight

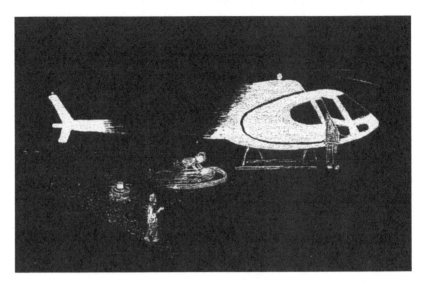

Rescue by torchlight

to safety. "Tell Alan about the cat," were his last words to Jake. "And give him all my stuff. And thanks heaps you guys. You're legends!"

They all watched the helicopter begin to hover then rise. Leaves and twigs flew up into their faces so they had to turn away with their hands over their ears. In a moment it was gone, its throbbing blades quickly receding into the night and its flashing red tail light disappearing into the low clouds.

Chapter 18

The Real World Returns

CAPTAIN BLIGH SPENT THE REST of the night on the island. He was a tough old fellow, and said he was quite happy to sleep in Rob's tent. But before they could go to bed that night there was so much to talk about. "Debriefing," Alan called it. "It helps get things out of our system," and he was right. As they sat around in the torchlight, all talking over the day's excitement and answering his many questions, it was as if a cloud was being lifted. Jess was back to her usual bubbly self, even giggling at his reaction when they told him his nickname.

"Captain Bligh, eh," he repeated with amusement. "It does have a nice ring to it. And I'm sure I deserved it, blaming you for something like that. Why didn't you tell me at the time that it wasn't your fire?"

"We tried to," shouted the three original castaways almost in unison, laughing.

"Maybe my hearing aid wasn't switched on," he murmured, before going on to question them about the activities at the salmon farm. "Don't worry," he assured them, "those men will never know how we found them out. Now we're onto them we can trace all their phone calls and track their movements. You might be surprised how many criminals we uncover through simple observations like yours. And it sounds like they deserve what they get. Are you sure they didn't lay their hands on you in any way, Jess? We might look into their dealings with internet photographs while we're investigating them."

"Are you in the police?" asked Fin curiously.

"Let's just say that I'm involved in law enforcement, but please don't spread it around," answered Alan. "And, by the way, you can call me Captain Bligh if you like!"

"There's another small thing I wanted to tell you," he said after they had laughingly chanted his nickname two or three times. "It's a bit more serious." They stopped their laughter and waited. "You see, I had a son once. He was a lot like you kids. He loved fishing and sailing and camping on this island, just like you." He paused, then continued, his voice breaking with emotion. "He went off to Afghanistan and never came back." There was another pause during which they sat in total silence, uncertain what they could say, but sharing his sadness.

Then his tone brightened. "He left behind his sailing boat, a yellow Mirror dinghy. I've got it still at my shack. I couldn't bring myself to sell it when he died." He paused again. "I'd like you kids to have it and share it however you think you can. I know you're from separate countries but you deserve to have as much fun in it as he had. It's one way I have of apologising for being such a ... such a Captain Bligh to you."

They all began talking, trying to tell him that they were sorry, that they had forgiven him, that he was a special friend now, but he got up. "Time I dossed down," he said cheerfully enough. "I'll see you all in the morning." And he was gone.

Once they were in their tents they continued to talk for a while. After an adventure like this, they were going to be friends for life. Zac and Tania talked about surfing in the freezing waters off Wellington's south coast while Jake and Jess tried to convince them that it was just as cold at Clifton Beach. Then they discussed school and how the Kiwi twins had a whole year's correspondence school lessons in boxes aboard *Moananui*.

"Even our science kits are in little boxes", said Tania.

"That's why we had to go back the other morning," added Zac. "Mum wanted us to start the first set."

They began making plans to spend the next few days sailing together in the channel, and Jake was sleepily telling them about his favourite anchorages when he heard Fin begin to snore. The conversation came to an end as one by one they relaxed into a deep and well-deserved sleep.

THE FIRST THING Jake became aware of next morning was the noise of an outboard somewhere in the distance. The second was the absence of any other noise, except for a few birds.

"Wake up, Zac, the wind's stopped," he said and wriggled out of the tent. The cat and its cage had gone, although Rob's bag and gun were still under the tent bivvy. Alan must have sneaked in and out quietly to avoid waking them up. In the background came another noise, the low rumble of a diesel engine and the clanking of anchor chain.

"They're here everyone! Get up," he yelled, pulling on his wet shoes. Zac was out in a flash, his long curly hair sticking out in all directions. Tania and Jess were a bit slower, crawling out one after the other and laughing at each other. They had slept in their clothes which were now crumpled and half untucked. Tania's hair had turned into long black ringlets from sleeping on it wet, and Jess's ponytail was loosened. They looked self-consciously at the boys until they realised that they were all equally messy. Fin heard them laughing, and wriggled out too, not quite sure what all the laughter was about.

The sun was shining through the trees to the east and the sky was blue overhead. Somehow the world seemed a wonderful place and their cares were over.

IT WAS A happy reunion when it came shortly afterwards. Even as both sets of parents were ferried ashore in *Moananui*'s grey inflatable, they could see Captain Bligh's punt returning across Privateer Strait (Jess's new name for it) with three boats in tow. One was white, one black and one yellow!

There was so much to tell their parents, so much laughter and even some tears. Strangely it seemed that it was the mothers who shed the most tears. Jim and Mike were talking like old friends rather than two men who had only met in Apollo Bay the previous stormy afternoon. Rose and Miriama kept looking at each other and smiling. They could see such a change in their children, as if they had suddenly grown years older.

"Don't worry, it's not an adult-free zone ever again," announced Jake as they made their way to Lighthouse Beach to meet Captain Bligh and their boats. They all laughed. The future looked so full of promise and there was still a whole week of sailing to do. Together.

Epilogue

THERE WAS SNOW ON MOUNT WELLINGTON, high above Hobart, as Jake led the way through the museum doors. He was in his best jacket and clutched the invitation in his left hand. The rest of his family followed, and after a brief conversation with the receptionist who smiled at him, they followed her instructions and filed up the stairs. Grandma went in the lift with his mother and they waited at the first floor for them. Grandma insisted on holding his arm and walking with him. She had her favourite red beret on her grey curls, and she winked at him as she opened the neck of her coat to show him the skull and cross-bones scarf he had knitted for her when he was eight.

"Shiver my timbers, it's the best thing to be wearing when buried treasure's revealed," she chuckled to him. They could hear the buzz of voices and even the clinking of wine-glasses as they approached the room. About twenty people were inside, some in suits. A man hurried up to Jake, nodded to his parents and led them to a tall grey man in a dark suit.

"This is the young man who found it," he said, and the man held out his hand. Jake had seen his picture before, the Governor of Tasmania.

"Jacob, is it? Pleased to meet you. One of my functions is to be patron of the museum. That's a significant piece of our history you have uncovered. Well done." He shook all their hands before being called away to talk to another man in a suit.

"Hi, Jake, fantastic to see you." It was Redbeard with Captain Bligh close by. "And Jess, and Fin. And you must be their parents. I hope you realise what an amazing bunch of kids you have here. And guess what, kids – there were three more forty-spots on the island at my last count!" He looked towards Grandma then, slightly uncertainly. Jake quickly introduced her and made her show him her scarf. "Grandma gave me *Privateer*'s sail," he explained. "She was a pirate too when she was young."

As Fin began excitedly telling Rob about the family's plans to rejoin their Kiwi friends later in the year, Alan quietly took Jake and Jess aside. "We've uncovered enough evidence on your so-called black-shirt visitors to put them behind bars for some time," he said, making sure no-one else could hear. "You'll probably read about it in the papers next week. But your involvement is only known to a handful of detectives. For your protection, no-one else will ever know your part in ..." But before he had finished, a hush came over the room. The museum curator walked towards Jake and led him to a long case hidden under a black cloth. He spoke briefly to the audience.

"Every now and then something significant is donated to our museum," he began. In this case it is thanks to Jacob Brownrig that this artefact was discovered. Usually such items are located by trained archaeologists, but in this case it was due to Jacob's persistence and perhaps intuition that the discovery was made. But what is even more remarkable is that he had the presence of mind not to simply pull it out of the ground and possibly damage it irrevocably as so many young people his age would have done. Instead he notified the appropriate authorities so that it could be correctly handled by our conservators."

There was a round of clapping, particularly loud and long, Jake noted, from his family and two new adult friends. The curator asked Jake to pull off the black cloth. There inside a glass case was a beautifully polished ancient muzzle-loading gun. The outline of its wooden stock was painted in the background. A plaque described what was contained in the case.

THIS MUSKET IS BELIEVED TO BE THE WEAPON USED BY ONE OF FOUR CONVICTS WHO, USING A STOLEN WHALEBOAT, INVADED THE COLE FAMILY HOMESTEAD ON SNAKE ISLAND IN 1840.
IN THE ENSUING FIGHT, THOMAS COLE AND HIS DAUGHTER, MARGARET, MANAGED TO DRIVE THE ATTACKERS OFF, ONE LATER DYING OF KNIFE WOUNDS.

IT WAS DISCOVERED AND DONATED
BY JACOB BROWNRIG.

Jake read the plaque and looked at the small crowd. He felt six feet tall.

ALSO BY JON TUCKER

Young Fin has always been passionate about fishing, so when he discovers an illegal net full of undersized fish in Sydney's northern waterways, his first reaction is to empty it. The subsequent events turn a joint Kiwi-Australian family holiday into a rather more complex experience.

Finalist for the Australian Environmental Award for Children's Literature, 2015

PRAISE FOR *THOSE ECO-PIRATE KIDS*

'In a complex and well-written tale of friendship and sailing, Jon Tucker gives a big nod to the tales of Arthur Ransome, while creating a modern-day adventure as thrilling as those books of older times. A clever and rewarding read.'

– Elizabeth Jolley (Editor, North Pole News – Oregon, USA)

'A highly enjoyable read ... which packs an emotional punch too. The wonderful relationships that develop between the children and the characters who start out as strangers show us how the world could be if people were to replace fear with careful assessment, reminding us of how much of what used to be normal we have lost. I must now join the list of people who are looking forward to the third book in the series.'

– David Cooper – Scotland (Amazon UK)

'Very antipodean and very Ransome at the same time as having a modern flavour, thus appealing to young children, aged parents and Ransome fans like me. I did find myself heading off to bed early (and getting up late) so I could find out what happened next. And for me, that is the sign of a good book.'

– Cheryl Paget – (Arthur Ransome Society literary journal – Mixed Moss)

For further information, visit www.nzmaid.com

ALSO BY JON TUCKER

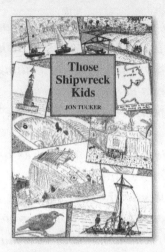

When a Tasmanian sailing family anchors near an old wrecked hulk in New Zealand's Marlborough Sounds, the kids discover a strangely abandoned campsite nearby, with plates of uneaten food and young children's toys still visible under the mould and cockroaches. Their curiosity leads to an investigation which adds a layer of intrigue to their anticipated fun-filled experiences in an unfamiliar foreign land.

A thought-provoking Ransome inspired tale with strong appeal to adventure-loving readers in the nine to ninety-nine age bracket. Underlying its clear environmental theme is the conclusion that freedom and responsibility go hand in hand.

PRAISE FOR *THOSE SHIPWRECK KIDS*

'A complex tale, realistic and fascinating, with characters we feel we know as real people. The reading level allows older elementary readers to enjoy the basic story line, but the depth of issues makes this a great read for teens and adults, too.'
– Elizabeth Jolley (Editor, North Pole News – Oregon, USA)

'The environmental message is clear, but not laboured, and is leavened by exciting contests between both the boats ... The mystery of the abandoned camp is finally resolved in a spectacular – if somewhat unexpected – denouement.'
– Mark Walker (Editor, Furthest South, magazine of
The Arthur Ransome Society in Australia and New Zealand)

'A sensible, inspiring story with plenty of practical information. It should be compulsory reading for every adventure loving kid.'
– Petr Baum (Czech Republic)

'In this third episode, the promise of the first two books is fulfilled. The characters are becoming more developed and the situations they deal with are more complicated. The increasing maturity of the kids allows Jon Tucker to explore more thoroughly the themes of independence and responsibility that were hinted at in the earlier books.

Jon Tucker writes in a deceptively straightforward way – the language may not be complex, but it manages to convey messages on several levels. I know I have to wait for episode 4, but I don't want to.'
– Jeremy M. Kriewaldt (Goodreads reviewer)

For further information, visit www.nzmaid.com

ALSO BY JON TUCKER

What happens when a couple of Kiwi kids who've been brought up with their brothers aboard a traditional ketch (with their own fleet of black pirate sailing dinghies), eventually grow up? When Ben Tucker and his youngest brother planned an expedition in search of the elusive South Magnetic Pole on Ben's small home-built sloop, their father Jon was allowed to join them as their cabin-boy, on a promise of good behaviour.

The unfolding true adventure took them through thick pack ice to become trapped at the windiest place in the world – Cape Denison, in remote East Antarctica. *Snow Petrel* is proof of what ordinary people can do with a minimum of money and a wealth of human spirit.

PRAISE FOR *SNOW PETREL*

'... an exceptional work from a gifted writer ... the story is so compelling that one wishes it not to end.'

– Janet Upcher, reviewer, Tasmania

'... a textured, intriguing, exhilarating story.'

– Rachel Edwards, book show host

'... up there with the best. Jon's writing style is perfect.'

– Don McIntyre, adventurer/columnist

*'**Snow Petrel** consists of two quite separate books. One is an extraordinary tale of sailing – well outside the genre of most sailing books. The second provides an insight into a very special family.'*

– Dr Nick Gales, Director, Australian Antarctic Division

For further information, visit www.nzmaid.com